喚醒你的英文語感！

Get a Feel for English !

喚醒你的英文語感！

Get a Feel for English !

難易：英檢中高至高級程度

翻譯大師

教你學寫作

高分修辭篇

作者／郭岱宗

大師獨門寫作要訣無私公開

大師獨門寫作要訣無私公開

- 大師以對照式學習法傳授實用高級用字與修辭技巧，立即提昇文字語句精確度，充分展現英文實力，作文自然得高分！
- 以實例帶領讀者漸進式學習寫作 know how：掌握「主旨」、充分發展「本文」、寫出精采「結論」，起承轉合全部到位！
- 從短文到長篇論文，掌握大師技巧，必能下筆自如！

Thesis statement:
A great sense of humor and loyal friendship exemplify my best friend, Tina.

Body:
發展 humor 和 friendship 的主軸

Conclusion:
Like a cellist plucks out an enchanting melody that can touch our souls, my soulmate plays her song with a friendly cheerfulness that enlightens my life.

貝塔語言出版
Beta Multimedia Publishing

IRT 語言測驗中心
Language Testing Center

口譯公式（The Formula of Interpreting）——郭岱宗

$$QI = EV + EK + FAAE$$

QI = **Q**uality **I**nterpreting（精於口譯）

EV = **E**ncyclopedic **V**ocabulary（豐沛的字彙）

EK = **E**ncyclopedic **K**nowledge（通達的見識）

F = Fluency（流暢）

| 流暢的字彙 | 流暢的句子 | 敏捷的反應 |
| 流暢的記憶 | 流暢的思路 |

A = Accuracy（準確）

| 發音準確 | 腔調準確 |
| 文法準確 | 譯意準確 |

A = Artistry（藝術之美）

| 文字之美 | 發音之美 | 台風之美 |
| 語調之美 | 聲音之美 |

E = Easiness（輕鬆自在）

金字塔理論：打造同步口譯的「金字塔」

（The Pyramid Theory of Simultaneous Interpretation）——郭岱宗

　　一切的翻譯理論，若是未能用於實際操作，都將淪為空談。優質的同步口譯超越了點、線、面，它就像一座金字塔，由下而上，用了許多石塊，每一塊都是真材實料，紮紮實實地堆砌而成。這些石塊包括了：

① 深闊的字彙

② 完整、優美、精確的譯文

③ 精簡俐落的句子

④ 迅速而正確的文法

⑤ 對雙文化貼切的掌握

⑥ 流暢的聽力

⑦ 字正腔圓

⑧ 優美愉悅的聲音

⑨ 適度的表情

⑩ 敏銳的聽眾分析和臨場反應

⑪ 穩健而親切的台風

　　最後，每一次口譯時，這些堆積的能量都隨點隨燃，立刻從金字塔的尖端爆發出來，這也就是最後一個石塊──快若子彈的速度！

　　這些石塊不但個個紮實，而且彼此緊密銜接、環環相扣、缺一不可，甚至不能鬆動。少了一角，或鬆了一塊，這個金字塔都難達高峰！

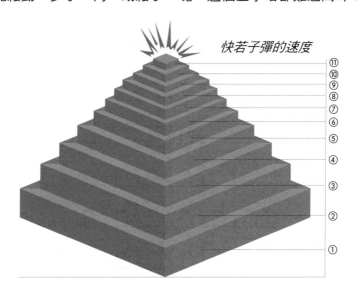

快若子彈的速度

漣漪理論（Ripple Theory）+ 老鼠會理論（The Pyramid Scheme）創造龐大且紮實的字彙庫──郭岱宗

字彙範圍須用「漣漪理論」：

記背單字不應採用隨機或跳躍的方式，而應該像漣漪一樣，由近至遠，一圈一圈，緊密而廣闊。

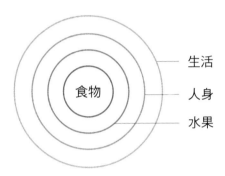

記背方法須用快速伸展字彙的「老鼠會理論」：

平日即必須累積息息相關、深具連貫性的字彙，口譯時才能快速、精確、輕鬆、揮灑自如！「由上而下」的「老鼠會式的字彙成長」，即以一個字為原點，發展為數個字，各個字又可繼續聯想出數個字。如此，一層層下來，將可快速衍生出龐大的字彙庫。既快速、有效、又不易忘記！

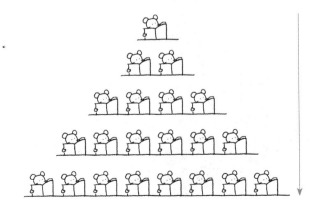

作者序

我們可以這麼看待英文寫作：它初步的價值在於**創作一個好作品**；它進一步的價值在於**讓作者有一個和自己心靈交會的機會**；而一篇好作品最大的價值則在於使**作者和讀者變的更好**。

寫出一篇優美的英文作文是一個腦力和感情兼用的工作，因為如果沒有深思熟慮，作品就沒有見解、欠缺深度；如果沒有置入感情，作品就難以扣人心弦、引起共鳴。

所以寫作與我們的心智相輔相成：只要專心一致地寫，任何一篇文章的寫作過程會使我們更成熟，因為我們的思緒變的更縝密、心靈變的更敏銳，因而理性與感性兼具。

這一本書教導如何寫高級英文作文。其實高級英文作文不過就是進階英文作文，一點也不難，只要遵循我在書中所提的方法，讀者可以在數個月之內，就得以掌握訣竅，一開始就能夠輕鬆地下筆，之後就有如千軍萬馬，氣勢難擋，最後則自然水到渠成，圓滿地收尾。

這本書將指出高級英文作文的特色，並用循序漸進的方式，帶著讀者一步一步寫作：先學高級英文作文該如何**鎖定方向**，然後學習如何**下筆**，之後學習如何**發展主文**，最後學習如何**收尾**，而每一次進展，都有**實例**帶領讀者學習英文創作。

學習首重方法，方法對了，自然就會了！感謝讀者與教學同仁使用本書，並敬祝各位健康順利。

郭岱宗

2010 年 5 月於淡江大學

前 言

在前書（翻譯大師教你學寫作——文法結構篇），我們已經學過英文寫作常用的基本句型以及英文作文的基本架構。在這一本書，我們將進一步討論難度較高的英文寫作，即所謂的高級寫作。

其實，高級英文作文並不難，只要遵循以下的寫作技巧，就可以從基礎英文寫作紮紮實實地進步到高級英文寫作：

1. 單字較成熟。

2. 句型較靈巧。

3. 邏輯較完整。

4. 思想較深邃。

5. 探討較具宏觀。

6. 文筆較細膩。

7. 氣勢較磅礴。

為了讓讀者更清楚地抓住重點，我用一個簡表來比較基礎英文作文以及高級英文作文的異同：

初級英文作文和高級英文作文的相同之處

1. 鎖定主題，打死都不離題，自始至終都圍繞著 main idea。就像一個孩子黏在母親身邊，無論怎麼走、怎麼繞，無論別處的誘惑有多大，都以母親為中心軸。

2. 不但用腦，也用感情，理性與感性必須兼具。正如一個「有腦無情」的男孩或女孩無論有多麼聰明和理性，仍會令人不耐，而「有情無腦」的人則缺乏致命的吸引力。

3. 起、承、轉、合，一個不少，才有邏輯。就像開車，若是突然啟動（因此起得不好）、隨時轉變（因此承得不好）、隨便轉彎（因此轉得不好）、隨意煞車（因此合得不好），都令人感到莫名其妙。

4. 文法正確，時態清楚，作文才讓人看得下去。

初級英文作文和高級英文作文的相異之處

	初級英文作文	高級英文作文
用字遣詞	比較幼稚	成熟靈巧
句型	比較簡單	精簡、有力、活潑
邏輯	合理	穩健而且精緻
結構	制式	靈活卻仍仔細融入「起、承、轉、合」
內涵	較淺薄	很有深度
文筆	平順	十分細膩、令人感動
氣勢	一般	令人震撼

　　看了以上這些標準之後，以下，我們一一來執行，一起把文章由初級英文作文蛻變為高級英文作文！

CONTENTS 目錄

Unit **1**

用字遣詞是化妝師

以下是英文作文中常見到的基本用語，我們就用它們來做例子，讓各位讀者一眼就知道如何立刻提昇英文寫作的用字遣詞。

 寫作的常用語

Part 1

（為了突顯這些用語的技巧，我們暫時使用十分口語而且淺顯的文字作例子。本書隨後會有嚴格而正式的訓練。）

	初級英文作文	高級英文作文
我認為	I think I believe I consider	**I'm convinced**（因為事實證明，而使人相信） **例** **I think** she is right. 　　↓ 改為 **I'm convinced** that she is right. 我完全相信她是對的。 **I deem**（視為） **例** **I regard** it as my responsibility. 　　↓ 改為 **I deem** it my responsibility. 我認為這是我的責任。 **I hold**（堅信） **例** **He believes** that she'll marry him. 　　↓ 改為 **He holds** that she'll marry him. 他相信她一定會嫁給他。

		Undeniably（無可否認地） 例 We **all consider** her as a good student. ↓ 改為 **Undeniably**, she is a good student. 我們絕對相信她是個好學生。
		Indisputably（無可置啄地） 例 It's out of the question that we **believe** this message cannot be wrong. ↓ 改為 This message is **indisputably** true. 這個訊息絕對錯不了。
我不認為	I don't think I don't believe I disagree	It's challengeable（可信度不高） 例 I **don't think** he is successful. ↓ 改為 His success is **challengeable**. 我不認為他是成功的。
		It's disputable（引人爭論的） 例 I **disagree of** his attitude. ↓ 改為 His attitude is **disputable**. 我不贊同他的態度。
		It remains doubtful（仍不可信） 例 I **still don't believe** that he'll marry her. ↓ 改為 **It remains doubtful** that he'll marry her. 我不相信他會娶她。

可是	but however nonetheless yet	有「比較」的意味：whereas 例 He is extroverted, **whereas** she is introverted. 他外向，可是她內向。
		有「沒想到」的意味：surprisingly 例 **Surprisingly**, she won! 但是她居然贏了！
		有「遺憾」的意味：unfortunately 例 **Unfortunately**, this was only a dream. 可是，這只是一場夢。
		有「事情不僅於此」的意味： accompanied by the fact 例1 He got married, but none of us expected that he would marry Jenny! ↓ 改為 He got married, **accompanied by the fact that** he married Jenny instead! 他結婚了，不過他娶的是Jenny！ 例2 Mary is an English major, and she is an outstanding student. ↓ 改為 Mary is an English major, **accompanied by the fact that** she is an outstanding student. 瑪麗是英文系的學生，而且十分優秀。

例如	for example for instance	A supporting fact is（有事實根據的例子） 例 He is happy—**a supporting fact is that** he smiles all the time. 他很快樂，**例如**，他臉上常掛著微笑。
		A sad fact is（令人難過的例子） 例 He is merciless—**a sad fact is that** he tortures animals. 他很無情，**例如**，他會折磨動物。
		A pleasant fact is（令人愉快的例子） 例 His efforts are rewarded—**a pleasant fact is** that he is graduating summa cum laude. 他的努力得到回報。**例如**，他即將以優異的成績畢業。 ※ summa cum laude (adv.) 以優異的成績…… [ˈsʊmə kʌm lɔd]
		A significant reason is（重要的例子） 例 Traveling is beneficial. **A significant reason is that** it enriches our lives and broadens our horizons. 旅行對人有益。**例如**，它豐富了我們的人生、擴展了我們的視野。
		A vivid example is（活生生的例子） 例 He babies her. **A vivid example is** he cooks for her everyday. 他寵愛她。**例如**，他每天為她下廚。

		An example comes to mind（我這就有一個現成的例子……）
		例 The National Palace Museum has an unprecedented advantage in capturing ancient Chinese culture. **An example**, the jadeite cabbage, **comes to mind**. 國立故宮博物院在保存古老的中國文化方面得天獨厚。翠玉白菜就是**一個現成的例子**。
另一個例子是	Another example is There's another example	This example doesn't stand alone（還有例子……） 例 第一個例子 + **This example doesn't stand alone.** + 第二個例子 例 Children can learn to respect animals under parental guidance. **A supporting fact is** that a child who is gentle with animals usually has parents who do the same. **This example doesn't stand alone**. A child who… 孩子經由父母引導而學習如何善待動物。例如，父母如果溫柔地對待動物，孩子通常也會這樣做。又例如，如果……
		This fact is supported by another example.（還有例子……） ※ 不過這些都屬「正面的」例子 例 第一個正面的例子 + **This fact is supported by another example**. + 第二個正面的例子

		A more insightful example is（還有例子⋯⋯）
		※ 不過例子「更深入」、「更有意義」
		例 第一個例子 ＋ **A more insightful example is that** ＋ 第二個例子
我永遠不會忘記	I'll never forget I'll always remember	An image that never slips from my mind is...（畫面永遠不會流逝） 例 **An image that never slips from my mind is** ＋ 敘述：the first time I saw a painting by Van Gogh in person.
		A memory that will never fade away is...（記憶永遠不會淡掉） 例 **A memory that will never fade away is** ＋ 敘述：the wonderful trip I took to Hokkaido with my family in 2008.
		A scene that shall always remain fresh is...（此景常新） 例 **A scene that shall always remain fresh is** ＋ 敘述：the day my best friend got married.

一、用字遣詞練習：

請嘗試用高級英文作文的用字遣詞，改寫以下句子。

1. I really think that he will succeed.

改為：＿＿＿＿＿＿＿＿＿＿＿＿＿＿＿＿＿＿＿＿＿

2. We all believe that he loves her.

改為：＿＿＿＿＿＿＿＿＿＿＿＿＿＿＿＿＿＿＿＿＿

3. I don't think boys are lazier than girls.

改為：＿＿＿＿＿＿＿＿＿＿＿＿＿＿＿＿＿＿＿＿＿

4. I love pets. For example, I have a cat and two dogs.

改為：＿＿＿＿＿＿＿＿＿＿＿＿＿＿＿＿＿＿＿＿＿

5. I love you, and I would die for you!

改為：＿＿＿＿＿＿＿＿＿＿＿＿＿＿＿＿＿＿＿＿＿

（以下答案只是參考，讀者可由書本中找出更多的進階用法）

1. I'm highly convinced that he will succeed.

2. Undeniably, he loves her.

3. It's disputable that boys are lazier than girls.

4. I love pets. A supporting fact is I have a cat and two dogs.

5. I love you, accompanied by the fact that I would die for you.

Part 2

	初級英文	高級英文
更何況	in addition, moreover, furthermore, besides,	…, let alone 例 … because I love her; **besides**, she is my only child. ↓ 改為 … because I lover her, **let alone** that she is my only child. 我……是因為我愛她，更何況她是我的獨生女。
		still less, 例 I don't mind assisting my students; **besides**, it's my responsibility. ↓ 改為 I don't mind assisting my students; **still less**, I'm fulfilling my responsibility. 我不介意幫助學生，更何況這是我的職責。
現在；目前	now today so far yet	to date 例 This work is not finished **yet**. ↓ 改為 This work is not completed **to date**. 這個工作至今尚未完成。

		at present
		例 **So far** 30 people have already come.
		↓ 改為
		Thirty people have arrived **at present**.
		目前來了三十人。
		※ 1. 在寫作中，0-9須拼英文字，10以上則使用阿拉伯數字。
		※ 2. 任何數字在句首都須拼出英文。
		at the present stage
		例 Let's wait and not reveal the crisis **yet**.
		↓ 改為
		Let's not reveal the crisis **at the present stage**.
		我們目前暫時不要揭露危機。
		Currently
		例 They are doing really well **now**.
		↓ 改為
		They are **currently** performing marvelously.
		他們目前表現得真好。
我的結論是	my conclusion is… to sum up,	In conclusion,
		例 **In conclusion**, + 句子
		結論是，……
		To summarize,
		例 **To summarize**, + 句子
		結論是，……

		To state succinctly, [sək'sɪŋktlɪ] 例 **To state succinctly**, + 句子 結論是，……
因為	because for	is ascribed to [ə'skraɪb] 例 He is successful **because** he has worked hard. ↓ 改為 His success can **be ascribed to** hard work. 他因努力而成功。´
		due to the fact (that) 例 He failed **because** he never tried his best. ↓ 改為 He failed **due to the fact** he never tried his best. 他因未盡全力而失敗。
停止	stop… quit	abstain from 例 He is trying to **quit** smoking. ↓ 改為 He is trying to **abstain from** smoking. 他正在努力戒菸。
習慣於	be used to	habitually 例 He **is used to** tolerating her. ↓ 改為 He is **habitually** tolerant of her. 他已習慣於容忍她。

		adapt (oneself) to
		例 We should try to **get used to** this teacher.
		↓ 改為
		We should **adapt ourselves to** this teacher. 我們應該去適應這個老師。
		例 Students should learn to **get used to** working quickly and assuming great responsibilities.
		↓ 改為
		Students must **adapt themselves to** working efficiently and taking responsibility. 學生應該習慣有效率以及有責任地做事情。
在⋯⋯方面特別	especially…	specialize in
		例 He is **especially** strong with numbers.
		↓ 改為
		He **specializes in** numbers. 他對數字很在行。
比⋯⋯好	better than	superior to
		例 His memory **is better than** mine.
		↓ 改為
		His memory **is superior to** mine. 他的記憶力比我強。

不比……好	worse than not better than	inferior to 例 My performance **is worse than** yours. ↓ 改為 My performance **is inferior to** yours. 我的表現比你差。
理當	… should…	supposedly 例 Students **should be** carefree. ↓ 改為 Students are **supposedly** carefree. 學生應該無憂無慮。 theoretically 例 Boys **should be** taller than girls. ↓ 改為 Boys are **theoretically** taller than girls. 男生應該比女生高。
根據報導	according to…	allegedly, 例 **According to** the newspaper, the birth rate is going down. ↓ 改為 **Allegedly**, the birth rate is declining. 根據報導，出生率在下降。

令我驚訝的是	to my surprise	surprisingly, 例 He didn't come. **What a surprise**! ↓ 改為 **Surprisingly**, he didn't show up. 他居然沒來，真令人驚訝！
我沒想到	I didn't know that I never knew sth. would happen	unexpectedly, 例 **I didn't know that** I could pass! ↓ 改為 **Unexpectedly**, I passed! 真沒想到，我居然過關了！
		had never expected (would happen) 例 **I never knew** we would fall in love. ↓ 改為 We fell in love, which **I had never expected**! 我從沒想到，我們居然戀愛了！

Exercise 2

一、用字遣詞練習：

1. You should forgive people; besides, she is your best friend.

改為：_____

2. So far we have 35 applicants.

改為：_____

3. We are trying to get used to this new rule.

改為：_____

4. She is especially good at TESOL.

改為：_____

5. Her performance is better than mine.

改為：_____

6. My English is no better than yours.

改為：_____

7. According to the newspaper, <u>the ruling party</u> won the election.

執政黨

改為：_____

8. To my surprise, <u>the opposition party</u> won the election.

反對黨

改為：_____

9. I didn't know that you were going to marry Tom.

改為：（已舉行婚禮）_____

改為：（尚未舉行婚禮）_____

10. If there are 10 <u>purchase orders</u>, we should be able to break the

訂單

record!

改為：_____

（以下答案只是參考，讀者可由書本中找出更多的進階用法）

1. You should forgive her, let alone that she is your best friend.

2. We have 35 applicants at the present stage.

3. We are adapting ourselves with this new rule.

4. She specializes in TESOL.

5. Her performance is superior to mine.

6. My English is inferior to yours.

7. Allegedly, the ruling party won.

8. Surprisingly, the opposition party won.

9. A: Unexpectedly, you married Tom!

    B: I never expected you would marry Tom.

10. Ten purchase orders would supposedly break the record.

Part 3

	初級英文	高級英文
極大的力量	with great strength	with the strength of several people 例 He lifts heavy objects **with great strength**. ↓ 改為 He lifts heavy objects **with the strength of several people**. 他用極大的力量抬重物。
在背後說人壞話	talk behind someone's back say bad things behind someone's back	smear [smɪr] 例 Don't **talk behind** my back. ↓ 改為 Don't **smear** me. 不要在背後中傷我。 --- malign [məˈlaɪn] 例 Don't **say bad things behind** his back. He is a very good person. ↓ 改為 Don't **malign** him—he's a good person. 他是一個有品格的人，不要說他壞話。

		vilify ['vɪlə.faɪ] 例 They often **say bad things about** her because they are jealous. ↓ 改為 They **vilify** her out of jealousy. 他們說她壞話是因為嫉妒。
百分百地保密	keep it 100% secret don't tell anyone	keep sth. strictly confidential 例 He **didn't tell anyone** about it. ↓ 改為 He **kept it strictly confidential**. 他沒告訴任何人。 maintain absolute secrecy 例 Please **promise not to let anyone know**. ↓ 改為 Please **maintain absolute secrecy**. 拜託完完全全保密！
任性而為	do whatever one wants to do	capricious [kə'prɪʃəs] 例 Parents should not spoil their children by letting them **do whatever they want to do**. ↓ 改為 Children should not be allowed to be **capricious**. 孩子不該被寵而任性。

活潑的	active	vibrant（活潑的、容光煥發的） 例 You look **vibrant** today. 你今天看起來容光煥發！
		animated（生動活潑的） 例 This story is quite **animated**. 這個故事很生動。
		lively（生命盎然的） 例 We had a **lively** discussion 我們熱烈討論。
		vivacious （有活力的） [vaɪˈveʃəs] 例 This old woman is **vivacious**. 這位老人充滿活力。

較長的寫作常用語

	初級英文	高級英文
事實上，並不……	in fact + 否定句 as a matter of fact + 否定句	there's no factual basis for… 例 **In fact**, this saying **isn't** true. ↓ 改為 **There's no factual basis for** this. 這一方面的觀點並不對。

我們都知……有害	We all know it's harmful to…	poses known hazards to… 例 **We all know it's harmful to** eat too much. ↓ 改為 Overeating **poses known hazards to** our health. 多吃有害。
事實證明，……	The fact proves that…	the evidence suggests (that) 例 **The fact proved** the prediction was correct. ↓ 改為 **The evidence suggested that** the prediction was correct. 事實證明，這個預測是正確的。
事實強烈地證明	The fact strongly proves	an undeniable fact can be found 例 **The fact strongly proves** that teaching is learning. ↓ 改為 **An undeniable fact can be found** in the expression, "teaching is learning." 教即是學，這是無庸置疑的。
必須決定輕重緩急	must decide what the most important thing to do first is	prioritize… 例 We must **learn to decide what the most important thing to do first is**. ↓ 改為 We must learn to **prioritize**. 我們必須學會事有先後。

和別人一起（吃社交飯）的時候	while we're (eating) with people for social contact.	in social (V-ing) 例 **While we're talking with people for the purpose of social contact**, we…. ↓ 改為 **In social communicating**, we… 當我們和別人進行社交方面的交談時，我們…… 例 **While we eat with people for the purpose of social contact**, we… ↓ 改為 **In social dining**, we…. 當我們和別人進行吃飯社交時，我們……
我們必須尊重別人，所以我們……	We must respect people, so we…	We…in due respect for others. 例 **We must respect people**, so we should wear suitable clothes. ↓ 改為 We are properly dressed **in due respect for others**. 為了尊重別人，我們的穿著需合宜。

如果我們……，就會……	If we…, we will…	… can be…
		
		例 **If we** are polite, **we will** be very popular.
		
		    ↓ 改為
		
		Courtesy **can be** winning.
		我們如果有禮貌，就會交到很多朋友。
		
		例 **If we** work hard, **we will** succeed.
		
		    ↓ 改為
		
		Hard work **can be** rewarding.
		我們如果有努力，就會成功！
		
		例 **If we** have faith, **we will** make it.
		
		    ↓ 改為
		
		Faith **can be** winning.
		我們如果有信心，就會成功！

如果我們從……的角度來看	If we look at it from the angle of…	from a… perspective
		
		例 **If we look at it from the angle of technology**, iPods are a great technological invention.
		
		    ↓ 改為
		
		From a technical perspective, iPods are a great technological invention.
		從技術的角度來看，iPod是一項很棒的科學發明。
		
		例 **If we look at it from the angle of money**, he is successful.
		
		    ↓ 改為
		
		From a financial perspective, he is successful.
		如果我們以金錢的角度來看，他是成功的。

		例 **If we look at it from the angle of the third person**, …. ↓ 改為 **From the third-person perspective**, …. 如果我們以第三者的角度來看，……
用 ⋮ 做 為 基 礎 ， ⋮	on the basis of …	on a foundation grown from... 例 **On the basis of** love, marriage can succeed. ↓ 改為 Marriage is optimal **on a foundation grown from** love. 婚姻如果**以愛為基礎**，就會成功。 例 Friendship grows strong **on the basis of** mutual trust. ↓ 改為 Friendship strengthens **on a foundation grown from** mutual trust. **以互信為基礎**的友誼是堅固的。

以上簡單地讓讀者看到，用字遣詞有不同的層次。隨後，在本書的「細膩的文筆帶來感動」一章，有更深入的例子供讀者練習使用。

Exercise 3

一、用字遣詞練習：

1. She rushed to rescue the child with great power.

改為：_____

2. She speaks with an active voice.

改為：_____

3. As a matter of fact, I don't think the estimate is reliable.

改為：_____

4. We all know that it's harmful to take drugs.

改為：_____

5. The fact proves that their hypothesis is absolutely correct.

改為：_____

6. We must respect others while we are talking to people for social contact.

改為：_____

7. We should care about students, so we should often talk to them.

改為：_____

8. Since parents should respect their children, we should listen carefully to them.

改為：_____

9. If you try to be happy, you'll get many things.

改為：_____

10. If we look at it from the angle of money, it's worthwhile.

改為：_____

參　考　答　案

（以下答案只是參考，讀者可由書本中找出更多的進階用法）

1. She rushed to rescue the child with the momentum of an avalanche.

2. She sounds animated.

3. There's no factual basis for this estimate.

4. Drugs pose known hazard to health.

5. An undiminished fact can be found in their hypothesis.

6. We must be respectful in social communicating.

7. Teachers constantly communicate with students in due concern for them.

8. Parents should listen attentively to children in due respect for them.

9. Cheerfulness can be rewarding.

10. It pays off from a financial perspective.

Unit 2

句型強烈展現
你的英文實力

多年來，我們所寫的英文句子一直不易擺脫中式英文。即使擺脫了，也並不順遂，因為我們難以自在地寫出俐落而精湛的句子。正因為這種桎梏，我們所寫的英文句子常顯累贅和軟弱，乏論美、力量，當然更缺乏吸引力。

 ## 何謂好句子？

1. 文法正確
2. 文字細膩
3. 語意清晰
4. 句子精簡並有力
5. 充滿魅力

我將隨後示範幾個初級英文以及高級英文的句子。英文的句型如果要真正脫胎換骨，就需要做大量經過專門設計的練習題。建議讀者可自行研讀「翻譯大師教你寫出好句子」，並認真做裡面的習題。

例1	他們不再活潑，而變的很僵硬。
基礎英文句	They are not active anymore, and they have become stiff.
	▼ 變
高級英文句	**Rigidity replaces animation.**

例2	他們失去了信心，而變的很畏怯。
基礎英文句	They have lost their confidence, and they have become timid.
	▼ 變
高級英文句	**Timidity replaces confidence.**

例3	他們不再精明，而變的猶豫不決。
基礎英文句	They are no longer sure, and they have become very hesitant.
	▼ 變
高級英文句	**Hesitation replaces shrewdness.**

例4	這一堂課，我們能用的語言，僅有英語。
基礎英文句	In this class, English is the only language we can use.
	▼ 變
高級英文句	**This class is conducted exclusively in English.**

例5	這個孩子不聽大人的話，而且目無尊長。
基礎英文句	This child neither listens to nor respects adults.
	▼ 變
高級英文句	**This child acts disobediently and disrespectfully.**

例6	從 2000 年到 2010 年，因為中國大陸的經濟愈來愈繁榮，人民幣升值了25%。
基礎英文句	From 2000 to 2010, because of China's increasing prosperity, the RMB has appreciated 25%.
	▼ 變
高級英文句	**The RMB had appreciated 25% from 2000 to 2010 due to China's unprecedented economic growth.**

例7	如果你今日夠努力的話，明日必有成功的果實。
基礎英文句	If you work hard enough today, you'll reap the fruit of success tomorrow.
	▼ 變
高級英文句	**Your efforts today shall be abundantly rewarded.**

例8	他再三地背叛她，這表示他們的婚姻大有問題。
基礎英文句	He has betrayed her over and over again, which shows they have serious marital problems.
	▼ 變
高級英文句	**His repetitive betrayals of her have revealed their marital crisis.**

例9	在八八水災之時，洪水和土石流滾滾而來，南台灣許多人死了，財產也喪失了。
基礎英文句	During the "August Eighth" disaster in southern Taiwan, floods and mudslides killed many people. Property was also lost!
	▼變
高級英文句	**Lives and property were taken by the floods and mudslides of the "August Eighth" catastrophe in southern Taiwan.**

例10	無論你有多累，都不該那麼做！
基礎英文句	No matter how tired you were, you shouldn't have done that!
	▼變
高級英文句	**Fatigue can't justify your behavior.**

例11	台灣四季分明，而且各有各的美。
基礎英文句	The four seasons are all different from one another, yet each has its own beauty.
	▼變
高級英文句	**Distinctive beauty is found in each of the four seasons in Taiwan.**

例12	台灣的春天花團錦簇、夏天艷陽高照、秋天秋高氣爽、冬天寒風凜凜，這四個季節也正好述說了大自然的生命。
基礎英文句	In Taiwan, different flowers bloom in spring; the sun shines bright in summer; the air is comfortable in autumn; and the winds are cold in winter. These four seasons describe the life of nature.
	▼ 變
高級英文句	**In Taiwan, the flowery springs, scorching summers, crisp autumns and freezing winters sound out the rhythm of nature.**

　　《翻譯大師教你寫出好句子》有更完整的訓練。讀者如果對於自己的造句有所期盼，亦請自行學習。

Exercise 4

一、請重新寫以下的句子：

1. If we stay honest, we will be trusted by people.

改為：＿＿＿＿＿＿＿＿＿＿＿＿＿＿＿＿＿＿＿＿

2. Even though you are angry, you can't just run away!

改為：＿＿＿＿＿＿＿＿＿＿＿＿＿＿＿＿＿＿＿＿

3. It's pathetic for a man/woman to forgive a wife/husband who has had a love affair.

改為：＿＿＿＿＿＿＿＿＿＿＿＿＿＿＿＿＿＿＿＿

4. They fought all the time, and they finally divorced.

改為：＿＿＿＿＿＿＿＿＿＿＿＿＿＿＿＿＿＿＿＿

5. They are deeply in love, very considerate to each other, and enjoy a very happy marriage.

改為：＿＿＿＿＿＿＿＿＿＿＿＿＿＿＿＿＿＿＿＿

6. After this accident, he is no longer confident in himself.

改為：＿＿＿＿＿＿＿＿＿＿＿＿＿＿＿＿＿＿＿＿

7. There's no reason for you to fail.

改為：_____

8. Without hope, life is fragile.

改為：_____

9. I don't mind if you are poor or not — I like you anyway!

改為：_____

10. It was so hot that many children went to the swimming pool to swim.

改為：_____

（以下答案只是參考，讀者可由書本中找出更多的進階用法）

1. Honesty wins people's trust.

2. Anger can't justify your escape.

3. Forgiven extramarital relations still heartbreak the spouse.

4. Frequent conflicts finally led to their divorce.

5. Their profound mutual love and consideration are blessed with a happy marriage.

6. This accident has deprived him of his self-confidence.

7. Your failure is inexcusable.

8. Hope strengthens life.

9. Your financial status is not an issue to me.

10. The high temperatures drove children to the swimming pool.

Unit 3

使文思如泉湧
－邏輯力量大！

曾經在國際新聞上看到一個北歐壯漢拉著一架飛機往前走嗎？就英文作文而言，邏輯的力量正是如此！邏輯的力量是如此之大，它在英文作文中，到底扮演什麼角色呢？

邏輯就是腦袋，我們的文章以何為主軸？源自何方？走向何方？如何走去？結果如何？力量如何？這一長串就譜成了文章的 **flow**。

因此，我們思緒的腳步行蹤必須十分穩定而清楚，這也正是寫作中不可缺少的起、承、轉、合。這四項得以譜成完整的邏輯，有了邏輯，文章得以自然發揮；因此不但使文意流暢，甚至使我們寫作的思緒「**一發不可收拾**」，自然「**水到渠成**」，整個寫作過程十分輕鬆。

提醒各位讀者，所有的好文章，無論屬何種型態，都必具有以下所列出的起承轉合，也就是一個清晰的思維所必掌握的邏輯性。（以下只是列表，讓讀者清晰地勾勒出文章的邏輯。至於如何執行，我們之後討論。）

 文章的結構

使文思如泉湧的簡表

起 Initiation	角色	用 thesis statement 寫出文章的 theme（主題），也就是第一段。
	目的	點出文章的主軸、立「起」整篇文章的方向。
	方法	用字遣詞必須引「起」讀者欲窺究竟的興趣。

承 Linkage	角色	文章的第二段，一直到結論之前的最後一段。
	目的	「承」起第一段的重點。
	方法	為了寫出深度與內涵，不能自說自話。可以用**事實**、**資料**、**訪談**、**數據**來支撐第一段的重點。

轉 Transitions	角色	如同蓋房子，磚頭不會一路砌上天，而需轉個彎，才會進入另一個房間，走入另一個境地。也如同畫畫，不會一筆拉個不停，而需轉個彎，才可畫出美麗的圖形。寫文章也完全一樣，在告一段落之後、如果還要續筆，之間也需要轉一下，才可圓順地走入下文。
	目的	使文章自然而優美地「**轉接**」。
	方法	善用**轉折語**或**過渡語**。

合 Conclusion	角色	為全文做一個「**合**」數。
	目的	再次強調**第一段**的重點，使文章的**論點**從頭到尾，完全一致。
	方法	順著主文（body）的氛圍，將文章的第一段主旨（theme）重新強調一次。
		它和主題句（thesis statement）一樣，用字遣詞字字珠璣、不可隨意，需嚴格注意修辭與意境，**氣勢要磅礴！**

Unit 4

起承轉合（一）
要「起」得巧

文章之「起」—— The Thesis Statement

英文寫作可真是名符其實地「萬事起頭難」。不過學習首重方法，如果方法不對，則搔破白頭、或是長篇大作，也難以寫出令人著迷的文章；反之，如果用對了方法，則可在數分鐘之內，輕鬆地下筆，並快速地完成，無論文章長短，均屬佳作。

理由很簡單，只要下筆得法，隨後而來的文思會因為「起」、「承」、「轉」、「合」的**連鎖反應**，而似泉湧，有若萬馬奔騰，勢不可遏。

換句話說，短短的 thesis statement 已幾乎決定這篇英文作文的成敗。

一個好的 **thesis statement**，必具備以下特色：

1. 清楚地點出全文的**主軸**：重點清楚、絕不含糊。
2. 奠定文章將走的方向：方向確定了，可令人一下筆就有如神助、思緒不斷、一氣呵成。
3. 雖然簡潔、清晰，卻不失完整：如果文章有三個重點，在 thesis statement 就必有三個關鍵字，一個不多、一個不少。
4. 生動活潑，引發讀者的**興趣**，有一窺究竟的慾望。
5. 用字遣詞成熟精湛。
6. 句型精簡有力。

以上是英文作文第一段的重點，我們在下筆練習之前，必須再進一步討論它的細節：

1. Thesis Statement 清楚地點出全文主軸

① Thesis statement 像一顆大樹的種子，也像一個廠的發電機，它是全文的生命源。

② Thesis statement 也就是全文的 theme，它帶著讀者直窺全文的核心與精神。

③ 每一個題目都可以因人而異而有不同的切入點，因而同一個題目會因為不同的作者而有不同的主題，我們要守住自己文章的主軸。
我們以 "Chinese Cuisine" 為例，它的主題可以是中國菜的歷史、或中國菜的烹飪特色、或外國人如何看待中國菜、或中國菜和義大利菜之異同……等等。所以，我們的主軸要抓住、思緒要過濾，不能把想到的全寫出來，因為腦筋裝的東西太多了，天馬行空會擾亂文章的中心思想，讓全文摸不清方向和重點。

2. Thesis Statement 不拘泥於固定的文體

首先，如果 thesis statement 沒抓好，任何的文體都不具意義。
絕對不要將自己綑綁於某種固定的文體，因為 thesis statement 是一個活潑、有力的生命體，我們可以用任何的文體來呈現它。例如，我們可以用「論說性」的文體，卻加上一首詩，就顯的剛柔並濟；也可以用「比較性」的文體加上充分的資料，就顯的嚴厲而客觀；當然也可以用「直述性」的文體，外加一則「新聞性」的報導，就顯的活潑且具深度。

3. Thesis Statement 可以「明示」，也可以「暗示」。

無論是「明示」或「暗示」，均需「確切」而「清楚」地指出全文的主軸。所謂「暗示」，即縱使它的內涵或關鍵字不那麼直接，卻能讓讀者心中極自然地期待讀到這篇文章所將闡釋的某些意旨。

4. Thesis Statement 必替下一段穩穩地鋪路。

只要腦中有料，我們的思緒是不會無緣無故斷掉的，所以，只要第一段（也就是 thesis statement）有重點，就已替下一段鋪好了路；換句話說，對作者而言，全文的走勢（flow）早已成竹在胸，完全掌控。所以第二段就水到渠成、欲罷不能、自然而然地延續下來，使全文順暢若流水。

5. Thesis Statement 雖然不長，卻具完整性。

雖然成熟的句子需精簡幹練、切忌冗長，但是 thesis statement 所發出的訊息仍必完完整整，缺一不可。在 thesis statement 之後的段落（也就是 body）之中，任何突發的重點，都將破壞文章的 **flow**；當然，會「突發」的原因即在於 thesis statement 有缺口、欠完整。

6. Thesis Statement 令讀者欲讀之而後快。

① 膚淺幼稚的字彙難以展現文字之美與巧。短短的 thesis statement 就像一顆鑲在皇冠上的鑽石，要發光發亮：它的用字遣詞不但優美，而且有力；不但呈現全文的主軸，而且精緻，讓讀者著迷。

② Thesis statement 也是一把鑰匙，將讀者引進一個神秘而美麗的花園。所以 thesis statement 不是空泛的、沒頭緒的，而是紮紮實實，並替文章孕育了豐富的靈魂和生命。

7. Thesis Statement 的句型成熟精湛。

Thesis statement 既是全文最主要的部分,句型豈可不慎?磨磨蹭蹭的句子必然堆出一個冗長、鬆散、甚至沒有重心的段落,不但不具吸引力,而且令人愈看愈累。所以, thesis statement 的句型必是精湛而有力的。

另外:

8. Thesis Statement 之前亦可加一個 lead。

Lead 是什麼?作用何在?怎麼才寫得好?這一方面的細節和練習,我們將隨後再討論。

我們一起提筆來「起」

文章如何下筆，一點都不可怕，因為寫作既是創作，就像畫畫、捏黏土、堆積木，應該是一件有趣的事情。一個活潑的題目固然較易寫出生動有趣的文章，但是，對於一個優秀的作者而言，如果把一個沉悶嚴肅的題目寫出一篇活潑生動的作品，就如同木雕藝術家把一塊再平淡不過的木頭雕成一個靈巧迷人的藝術品，完成一個快樂的挑戰。

我們該這麼想：文章是人寫出來的，我們的頭腦本來就不該受制於題目，而是**題目被我們活化**。再枯燥、通俗的題目，碰到活潑的頭腦，都可以寫出令人讀之難忘的作品。

其實，初級英文寫作和高級英文寫作的文章結構和邏輯都是一樣的，只是高級作文因為文字、句型、思緒都更靈巧而且更具彈性，所以文章必然更活潑、充實、且更具深度。現在，為了帶著讀者清楚地由初級英文寫作進階到高級英文寫作，我特意找出平時極常見的、亦即十分平凡的作文題目，並且示範，初級作文和高級作文即使寫同樣的題目，甚至寫同樣的內容，兩者的 thesis statement 卻不盡相同。我們一起來試試看。

第一個題目：My Best Friend

如果 thesis statement 這麼寫
Everyone has good friends, and so do I! My best friend is...
缺點： 1. 乏味（只是複誦題目而已，不具意義） 2. 陳腔濫調（缺乏主見） 3. 沒有重點（太廣泛了，流於空洞），浪費篇幅！ 4. 所以找不到關鍵字。 5. 因此沒有指出文章的方向。 6. 用字膚淺。 7. 句子鬆散。

↓ 這樣較好

初級英文作文的 thesis statement 這麼寫

My best friend is **Tina**, who is very **humorous** and is very **nice** to me.

有優點了： 1. 指出了全文發展的方向：我最好的朋友是幽默而友好的。

2. 有關鍵字： humorous, nice

還是有缺點： 1. 用字幼稚。

2. 太呆板、完全不生動。

3. 未能塑造意境。

↓ 一模一樣的內容，
這樣寫就會立刻踏入高級英文作文

高級英文作文的 Thesis Statement

Humor and **friendliness** exemplify my best friend, **Tina**.

1. 關鍵字清楚： humor, friendliness, Tina。

2. 因此文章的主軸穩定明朗。

3. 字彙成熟有力。

4. 句型精湛俐落。

5. 動詞使用 "exemplify"，使文章活起來。

第二個題目：My Mother

如果 thesis statement 這麼寫
I have a great mother, who loves us so much that she works very hard all the time.
缺點：1. 陳腔濫調（絕大多數的母親皆如此）。 2. 沒有重點（太廣泛了，流於空調）。 3. 所以找不到關鍵字。 4. 用字膚淺。 5. 句型鬆散無力。 6. 沒有指出文章的方向。

↓ 這樣較好

初級英文作文的 thesis statement 這麼寫
My mother is a **housewife**. She is very **smart** and not only **loves** us, but **other children** as well.
有優點了：1. 有關鍵字： housewife, smart, love(s) other children。 　　　　　2. 指出全文發展的方向：幼吾幼以及人之幼。 還是有缺點：1. 用字幼稚。 　　　　　2. 意境未能深入人心。 　　　　　3. 句型鬆散。

↓ 一模一樣的內容，
　這樣寫就會立刻踏入高級英文作文

高級英文作文的 Thesis Statement
The **intelligence** and **altruistic maternal** love of my mother compliment her role as a **housewife**.

1. 關鍵字清楚： intelligence, altruistic, housewife。
2. 因此文章的主軸已穩固、明朗。
3. 字彙成熟有力： intelligence 代替 smart ；
   altruistic 代替 loves other children ；
   maternal love 代替 she loves us。
4. 句型精緻俐落。
5. "compliment her role as…" 使文章活潑起來。
6. 「刻畫母親」的意境呈現。

第三個題目：My Definition of Beauty

如果 thesis statement 這麼寫
There are different kinds of beauty. For example, many young people are beautiful, but some old people are also very beautiful. Therefore, age is not a factor of beauty.
優點：點出了文章的方向：美不受年齡的限制。 缺點： 1. 字彙淺薄。 　　　 2. 句型鬆散。

這樣較好

初級英文作文的 thesis statement 這麼寫
Young or old, a person can be beautiful. It's true that children are lovely, but old people are also beautiful, especially if they have a kind heart.
優點：更精確地指出全文的方向：老年人的慈愛之美。 缺點： 1. 字彙淺薄，沒有份量。 　　　 2. 句型軟弱，沒有力量。

一模一樣的內容，
這樣寫就會立刻踏入高級英文作文

高級英文作文的 Thesis Statement
Genuine **generosity**, true **mercifulness** and unchallengeable **wisdom** accent the charisma of **old age**—the image of real beauty.

1. 關鍵字清楚： generosity, mercifulness, wisdom, old age
2. 因此確切地點出全文將發展的方向： ① 大方 ② 慈愛 ③ 有智慧是老年之美，也是真正的美。
3. 字彙成熟有力。
4. 句子精簡。
5. "accent the charisma of old age" 為文章加入生命，動詞使用 "accent"，句子立刻活潑起來。
6. 意境呈現。

　　我們接下來跳過失敗的例子，直接進入初級英文作文與高級英文作文的比較。

第四個題目：On Mixed-Cultural Marriages

初級英文作文的 theme 這麼寫
"I want to eat dumplings!" versus. "I want to eat beefsteak!" Or "Let's visit my parents today!" versus. "Why? You are married and should be indepemdent from your parents!" These conflicts may frequently happen in mixed-cultural marriages.
優點： 1. 有關鍵字： cultural conflicts。 　　　 2. 鎖定主題：異國婚姻時有衝突。 　　　 3. 指出文章發展的方向：異國婚姻常在飲食和家庭方面有歧見。 缺點： 1. 用字較幼稚。 　　　 2. 關鍵字太少。 　　　 3. 那兩句對話放在 thesis statement 太浪費篇幅；應該放在 **body**， 　　　　 用來支撐 **theme**。

一模一樣的內容，
↓ 這樣寫就會立刻踏入高級英文作文

高級英文作文的 Thesis Statement
Mixed-cultural marriages face unavoidable **conflicts**, ranging from **cuisine** to **family values**.
1. 關鍵字清楚： conflicts, cuisine, family values。 2. 因此全文的主軸已穩固、明朗。 3. 字彙成熟。 4. 句型俐落。 5. "face unavoidable conflicts" 使文章活潑起來。 6. 意境呈現。

Exercise 5

我們一起來練習文章之「起」。為了清楚地比較，我們假設在一個題目之下文章的方向和內容也完全一樣的，只是 thesis statement 寫得好與不好而已。

題目：**1. 以下哪一個thesis statement最好？**

2. 請依優劣排名1、2、3。

3. 排名的原因為何？

Topic 1: My Favorite Song

	Thesis Statement
排名	My favorite song is *Beauty and the Beast* because it has a beautiful melody, and the singer has a deep, attractive voice. 原因：
排名	I believe my favorite song is *Beauty and the Beast.* The first time I heard it in the movie theater, I was immediately attracted to it. 原因：

排名	An enchanting melody and romantic lyrics sung with a characterize voice compose my favorite song: *Beauty and the Beast*. 原因：

Topic 2: The Definition of Success

	Thesis Statement
排名	Is a man successful when he is rich? Is a man successful when he is famous? Are we successful when we have a high degree? Are we successful when we have a god job? 原因：
排名	What is real success? In our society, many people pursue money, careers and degrees so hard that I really doubt they are truly happy. 原因：

排名	Wealth, fame or high education are not equivalent to success when they are not accompanied by happiness. 原因：

Topic 3: The Value of Forgiveness

	Thesis Statement
排名	No one is perfect, which makes it human and reasonable to forgive people's mistakes. 原因：
排名	Even an honest person may tell a white lie and even a merciful person may accidentally hurt people. Shouldn't people be forgiven when they make mistakes? 原因：
排名	Forgiveness can be as virtuous as honesty and mercifulness. 原因：

Topic 1: My Favorite Song

	Thesis Statement
排名 2	My favorite song is *Beauty and the Beast* because it has a beautiful melody, and the singer has a deep, attractive voice. **優點**：有關鍵字（可以鎖定主題）： *Beauty and the Beast*; beautiful melody; voice 所以知道全文的發展方向將是這首歌的美麗旋律和動人聲音。 **缺點**：1. 用字遣詞不夠優美。 　　　　2. 句型還須加油。
排名 3	I believe my favorite song is *Beauty and the Beast*. The first time I heard it is the movie theater. I was immediately attracted to it. **缺點**：1. 沒有主題：只知道是 *Beauty and the Beast* 這一首歌，但是全無重點，文章將走向何方？沒有鎖定。 　　　　2. 文字須加油。 　　　　3. 句型須再努力。

排名	An enchanting melody and romantic lyrics, sung by a characterize voice compose my favorite song: *Beauty and the Beast*.
1	

優點： 1. 有關鍵字（所以主題已鎖定）：

　　　　 melody; lyrics; voice; *Beauty and the Beast*

　　　 2. 用字遣詞較成熟。

　　　 3. 句型簡潔有力：全段只須一個句子，意義就十分完整，而且充滿生命力。

Topic 2: The Definition of Success

	Thesis Statement
排名	Is a man successful when he is rich? Is a man successful when he is famous? Are we successful when we have a high degree? Are we successful when we have a god job?
3	

優點：主題清楚：「有金錢」、「有名」、「高學位」、「好工作」，不見得就是成功！

缺點： 1. 用字隨便。

　　　 2. 句子太囉唆。

排名	
2	What is real success? In our society, many people pursue money, careers and degrees so hard that I really doubt they are truly happy.

優點：主題鎖定得更清楚：如果不快樂，一切的金錢和成就都枉然。

缺點：1. 句子鬆散。

2. 用字須再努力

排名	
1	Wealth, fame or high education are not equivalent to success when they are not accompanied by happiness.

優點：主題和上一個一樣，清楚地鎖定方向，但是：

1. 用字遣詞較成熟。

2. 句型簡單俐落，句意更清楚。

Topic 3: The Value of Forgiveness

	Thesis Statement
排名	No one is perfect, which makes it human and reasonable to forgive people's mistakes.
3	

缺點：雖已鎖定主題，但仍不夠精準（precise），不知文章將走的方向為何？

排名	Even an honest person may tell a white lie, and even a merciful person may accidentally hurt people. Shouldn't people be forgiven when they make mistakes?
2	

優點：主題清楚地鎖定：連誠實、慈善的人都會犯錯，我們怎能不
　　　　原諒人呢？

缺點：1. 文字不夠成熟。

　　　　2. 句型須再努力。

排名	Forgiveness can be as virtuous as honesty and mercifulness.
1	

優點：1. 主題清楚：「誠實」、「慈悲」是美德，「寬恕」的這種
　　　　情操和兩種美德比起來毫不遜色。

　　　　2. 字彙成熟。

　　　　3. 句型俐落有力。

Unit 5

起承轉合（二）
要「承」得準

文章之「承」——The Body

寫完第一段（thesis statement）之後，立即接著寫主文（body）。所謂「承」，即文章的 body 「承擔」上一段所提及的所有重點。這真的很簡單，因為在 **thesis statement** 中的每一個關鍵字，都至少可寫出一段文章，而這全部的段落加起來，就是全文的 **body**。

請看以下圖表，即可了解英文作文當中的「起」和「承」之間的關係。

英文作文如果只寫 1~2 頁

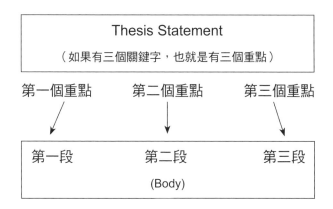

算算段落：

    1 段（Thesis Statement）

    3 段（Body）

+   1 段（Conclusion）
    ─────────────────
    5 段（全文）

英文作文如果寫 2~4 頁

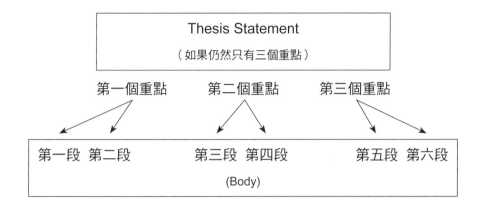

算算段落：

$$1 段（Thesis Statement）$$
$$6 段（Body）$$
$$+ \quad 1 段（Conclusion）$$
$$\overline{}$$
$$8 段（全文）$$

英文作文如果寫 4~6 頁

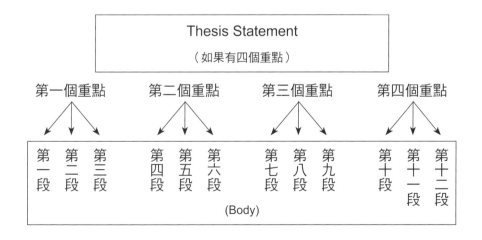

算算段落：

$$
\begin{array}{r}
1 \text{ 段（Thesis Statement）} \\
12 \text{ 段（Body）} \\
+ \quad 1 \text{ 段（Conclusion）} \\
\hline
14 \text{ 段（全文）}
\end{array}
$$

　　英文作文的長短其實伸展自如。在 thesis statement 當中，關鍵字（也就是重點）可以增減，而在主文（body）當中，每一個重點所發揮出來的段落數目也可以增減。如此類推，再多的字數均可輕鬆搞定。

　　我們依照以上的邏輯，就可以在 body 中，活潑地操控 thesis statement 所寫到的每一個重點。例如，一個重點（關鍵字）就可揮灑出一個至許多個段落。

　　我們以 thesis statement 有三個重點為例：

Thesis Statement ▼ Body	第一個重點 ▼	第二個重點 ▼
	第一段：例子 + 第二段：另一個例子 + 第三段：訪談	第一段：例子 + 第二段：另一個例子 + 第三段：訪談

　　以上，一個重點就可寫出三個段落；如果 thesis statement 只有兩個重點，主文就已經有六段了，再加上 thesis statement 和 conclusion，全文就一共有八段了。

文章既是活的， body 當然也可這樣寫：

Thesis Statement ▼	第一個重點 ▼	第二個重點 ▼
Body	第一段：例子 + 第二段：例子 + 第三段：自己的判斷	第一段：例子 + 第二段：例子 + 第三段：自己的判斷

作文如果還要再長，則可**正面**和**反面**均加以討論，亦即：

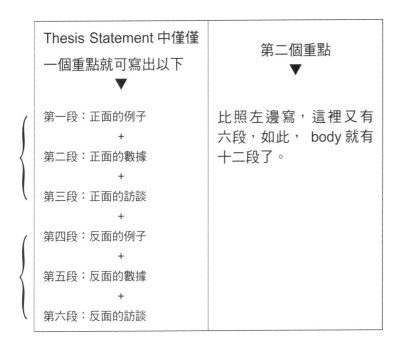

Thesis Statement 中僅僅一個重點就可寫出以下 ▼	第二個重點 ▼
第一段：正面的例子 + 第二段：正面的數據 + 第三段：正面的訪談 第四段：反面的例子 + 第五段：反面的數據 + 第六段：反面的訪談	比照左邊寫，這裡又有六段，如此， body 就有十二段了。

又如，我們假設 thesis statement 中有三個重點：

Thesis Statement ▼	第一個重點 ▼	第二個重點 ▼	第三個重點 ▼
Body	第一段：例子 + 第二段：另一個例子 + 第三段：數據	第四段：例子 + 第五段：另一個例子 + 第六段：數據	第七段：例子 + 第八段：另一個例子 + 第九段：數據

↓ 如果作文需要更長

Thesis Statement ▼	第一個重點 ▼	第二個重點 ▼	第三個重點 ▼
Body	第一段：例子 + 第二段：另一個例子 + 第三段：集合別人的觀點（或是文獻資料、訪談） + 第四段：數據	第五段：例子 + 第六段：另一個例子 + 第七段：集合別人的觀點（或是文獻資料、訪談） + 第八段：數據	第九段：例子 + 第十段：另一個例子 + 第十一段：集合別人的觀點（或是文獻資料、訪談） + 第十二段：數據

如果還要繼續加長，
還可在 thesis statement 增加重點，
使文章更有內涵

Thesis Statement ▼	第一個重點 ▼	第二個重點 ▼	第三個重點 ▼	第四個重點 ▼
Body	第一段：例子 + 第二段：另一個例子 + 第三段：集合別人的觀點（或文獻資料、訪談） + 第四段：數據	第五段：例子 + 第六段：另一個例子 + 第七段：集合別人的觀點（或文獻資料、訪談） + 第八段：數據	第九段：例子 + 第十段：另一個例子 + 第十一段：集合別人的觀點（或文獻資料、訪談） + 第十二段：數據	第十三段：例子 + 第十四段：另一個例子 + 第十五段：集合別人的觀點（或文獻資料、訪談） + 第十六段：數據

如果繼續加長

Thesis Statement ▼	第一個重點 ▼	第二個重點 ▼	第三個重點 ▼	第四個重點 ▼
Body	第一段：例子 + 第二段：文獻或訪談 + 第三段：數據 + 第四段：另一個例子 + 第五段：文獻或訪談 + 第六段：數據	第七段：例子 + 第八段：文獻或訪談 + 第九段：數據 + 第十段：另一個例子 + 第十一段：文獻或訪談 + 第十二段：數據	第十三段：例子 + 第十四段：文獻或訪談 + 第十五段：數據 + 第十六段：另一個例子 + 第十七段：文獻或訪談 + 第十八段：數據	第十九段：例子 + 第二十段：文獻或訪談 + 第二十一段：數據 + 第二十二段：另一個例子 + 第二十三段：文獻或訪談 + 第二十四段：數據

所以，只要增加 thesis statement 的關鍵字，就可增加段落。因此只要**言之有物，文章應該愈長愈有內涵。**

同時，每一段也可自行調整內涵。

例如：用**正面**的例子來支持我們的觀點。

用**反面而失敗**的例子來支持我們的觀點。

用**現代**的例子來支持我們的觀點。

用**歷史**的例子來支持我們的觀點。

用**名人**的看法來支持我們的觀點（interview 或看書、上網查資料）。

如果找到**數據**支持（以及數據的來源），我們的**論點會更專業**。

也可用**幻想**或**假設**另立文章的立足點。

然後用事實來肯定以上這個立足點。

以上輕輕鬆鬆，不用絞盡腦汁，文章就可以順著發展，而且作品不但絕對不會偏離主題、又具內涵，且合邏輯，當然也具有可信度。

如果文章還要長而不失邏輯，以上的例子、數據、訪談均可各再用不同的資料，各加一段，即每個重點都為 body 再帶來一倍的長度；如果還要再長，可以在綜合各種資料和別人的觀點之後，每一個部分都再加上一段自己的討論，就又多了好幾段；如果還要再長，我們也可以繪製表格，文章將更具科學與專業價值，亦走往論文的領域。

文章的長短可短自數十字，長至數十萬字。但是，**無論長短，均需字字珠璣、鎖定主軸、不可偏離**。文章只要「起」得好，「承」得準，愈長的文章只有更加細膩深邃。反之，文章如果「起」得不好，或「承」得不準，則勢必天馬行空、愈長愈空洞，輕則索然無味，重則令人讀之而感覺不知所云。

我們在前面已經討論了 body 的任務和內容，現在我們來看看它所涵蓋的段落當中，每一段內容的**結構**（長相）如何。

主文（Body）的架構

首先，body 立即順勢出現在 thesis statement 之後，因為 thesis statement 早已替它鋪好了一條順暢之路。

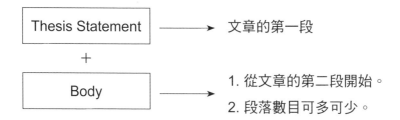

Thesis Statement	→ 文章的第一段
+	
Body	→ 1. 從文章的第二段開始。 2. 段落數目可多可少。

Body 既然「承」起了 thesis statement，也就是要承接（bolster）第一段（主題）的各項重點，所以它的結構必然穩健而紮實，否則這個 body 東倒西歪的，如何承擔重任？

英文作文中，**思路清晰、邏輯通順**的 body，必有以下的結構：

Body 中的每一個段落均包括：	topic sentence：它在這一段的地位，就如同 thesis statement 在全文的地位。因此，它就是這一段的主題。
	小 body：它在這一段的地位，就如同主文（body）在全文的地位。為了方便討論，我在本書中將把全篇文章的主文稱為大 body，一段當中的主文則稱為小 body。
	main point：它在這一段的地位，就如同 conclusion 在全文的地位。因此，它就是這一段的**結論**。

就以上的簡表，我們來討論大 body 中的每一個段落的細節：

第一部分：Topic Sentence

一篇作文的 body 中的**每一個段落都是一個迷你而完整的世界**，正如同我上面所列出的簡表，**每一段都像一篇小作文**，各有自己完整而獨立的意念。

因此，它有自己的 thesis statement，只是名稱改了，被稱為 topic sentence （主題句），顧名思義，它指的就是這一段的 topic，必須展現這一段的主題（theme）。**它既是主題，必也有關鍵字，而且關鍵字必須清晰而有力，才能替隨之而來的小 body 鋪路。**

第二部分：小 Body

這一段的開頭既然已有 topic sentence，接著就要用小 body 來承擔 topic sentence 中所提的重點，它的作用和全篇作文的大 body 完全一樣。在這一段當中，也有清晰的邏輯：topic sentence 為「起」、小body 為「承」，也因為有邏輯，這個段落亦自然擁有圓順的 flow。

和大 body 的功能一樣，這個小 body 可用例子、數據、理論來支持 topic sentence。當然，再次提醒，**例子要活潑生動，文章才有生命。**

第三部分：Main Point

大 body 的每一個段落，因為自有其完整性，所以在每一段當中除了主題（topic sentence）、小主文（body）之外，也必須有結論。不過，全篇作文的結論叫做 conclusion，一個段落中的結論則改稱為 main point。

Main point 在段落中的作用和 conclusion 在全文中的作用一模一樣：文章自 theme 開始，經由 body 所呈現的種種細節之後，在這裡又再回到 theme 的重點。這個結論就好像說：看吧！我的立場「自始至終」都完全

一致，沒有偏離，也沒有自相矛盾；甚至在每一段之中，邏輯也都是「前後一致」、「思路穩健」！

因此，在大 body 之中，每一個段落之內的邏輯，和全文的邏輯完全相符，我們看以下就會更清楚了：

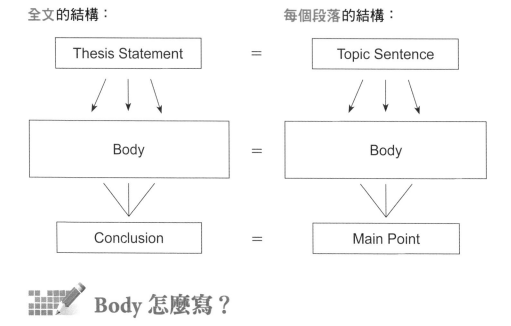

全文的結構：　　　　　　　　　　**每個段落**的結構：

Thesis Statement	=	Topic Sentence
Body	=	Body
Conclusion	=	Main Point

Body 怎麼寫？

文章在 thesis statement 之後，即是主文。我們延用之前的作文題目和 thesis statement，示範如何繼續寫下去，body 寫得又快又好。

題目： My Best Friend

<table>
<tr><td colspan="2" align="center">**Thesis Statement**</td></tr>
<tr><td colspan="2">Like how a beautiful melody and classic lyrics interweave to create an intoxicating song, a great sense of **humor** and loyal **friendship** exemplify my best friend, **Tina**.</td></tr>
<tr><td colspan="2">關鍵字： humor, friendship, Tina</td></tr>
</table>

 進入主文

大 Body 的第一段（Humor Part 1）		
使用例子	topic sentence	It's never hard to locate Tina among a group of people.
		關鍵字： locate、Tina
	小 body	舉例來支撐並刻劃這一段的 topic sentence ： 1. Tina 遼闊的笑聲 2. Tina 在人群中的光環 3. Tina 開朗的行為
	main point	It's a true blessing that someone can be so filled with genuine **happiness** like Tina.
	解析： 1. 因為小 body 中已有快樂的例子，所以它助使結論（main point）水到渠成，自然引向 happiness。 2. Main point 中的 "happiness" 回應 topic sentence 的主題： 她如此開朗快樂，在人群中很難找不到她。	

大 Body 的第二段（Humor Part 2）		
使用資料	topic sentence	The Bible says, "**A cheerful heart** is good medicine," and Tina **vividly** displays this trait.
	小 body	從書本、研究、媒體、網路查出開心對健康有益的資料或數據，使文章更專業。
	main point	The figures have explicitly explained why Tina is always so **dynamic**.

解析：

1. 小 body 中所提供的資料，解釋 topic sentence 中的 a cheerful heart 的確讓 Tina 神采飛揚；之後，使結論（main point）水到渠成，邏輯順暢、flow 自然就圓潤了。

2. 結論中的 "dynamic" 和 "vividly" 是氣勢相合，也回應 topic sentence 的主題：喜樂的心乃是良藥！喜樂勝於一切！

大 Body 的第三段（Friendship Part 1）		
使用資料	topic sentence	既然上一段用古老的語錄開啟（A cheerful heart is good medicine），如果這一段也用同樣的意境和格式，文章即展現文字的平衡之美。這種機會不是每次都有，但是只要可能，就不要放過。
		"A hedge between keeps friendship green," realistically illustrates my friendship with Tina.
	小 body	舉例來支撐並刻劃這一段的 topic sentence，「君子之交淡如水、水長流」。這一方面的例子很多，所以很有的發揮。例如可描述，我和 Tina 雖不是如影相隨，但是我們的友誼長存。
	main point	Indeed, our friendship stands up to the challenges of both time and space.
解析： 1. Main point 的意義是「我們的友誼禁得起時間和空間的考驗」，正完全呼應這一段的 topic sentence （君子之交淡如水、水長流）。 2. 因為小 body 描述我和 Tina 友誼長存，所以結論自然水到渠成，而且邏輯順暢、flow 圓潤。		

+

大 Body 的第四段（Friendship Part 2）		
使用資料	topic sentence	The friendship between Damon and Pythias has been eulogized for ages, and is echoed among similar friendships today.
	小 body	從媒體、書本、網路查詢在現今社會中，堅強友誼的資料或數據。
	main point	The striking figures have extolled the value of true friendship.
	解析： 1. 小 body 所提供的資料使結論自然水到渠成。 2. Main point 的意涵是「令人領悟真友誼的價值」，也完全呼應這一段的 topic sentence ：「Damon and Pythias 之間的真友誼，至今仍有」。	

在初級英作中，我們因為寫作的經驗不足，所以 body 的結構須完全遵守、十分嚴謹，何況全民英檢或托福等任何的英文能力鑑定考試的作文評分標準都完全鎖定這個格式，提醒各位讀者不可離開這個架構。

不過，在高級英文或專業的英文寫作（例如新聞英文或是 feature story）中，則「邏輯依舊，架構卻更靈活！」

其細節及方法，等我們做完這一章的練習之後，在下一章，「轉」的部分來討論。

Exercise 6

請先看thesis statement的關鍵字，然後由不同段落的主題當中，判斷哪一段的內容會破壞大body的「承」的工作？

題目 1.

作文題目	**Key Words** in Thesis Statement
Cynicism and Health （憤世妒俗與健康）	stress（壓力） interpersonal relationships（人際關係） cancer（癌症） appreciation（感恩與珍惜）

根據作文題目與 key words，下列的段落主題若出現在大 Body 中是否適當？為什麼？

這一段落的主題是：	適合嗎？	不可取的原因
The importance of exercise	Yes / No	
How cynicism may cause stress	Yes / No	
Theories or experiments supporting how cynicism may cause stress	Yes / No	
How stress may cause cancer	Yes / No	
Statistics showing major causes of cancer	Yes / No	
A fact showing how cynicism affects interpersonal relationships	Yes / No	
Wise sayings supporting how appreciation helps avoid cynicism	Yes / No	

Experiments or statistics showing appreciative people tend to live longer	Yes / No	

題目 2.

作文題目	**Key Words** in Thesis Statement
The Boughs That Bear Most Hang Lowest （肚大才能容）	humility（謙卑） tolerance（容忍） forgiveness（寬恕）

根據作文題目與 key words，下列的段落主題若出現在大 Body 中是否適當？為什麼？

這一段落的主題是：	適合嗎？	不可取的原因
An example showing how humility allows for more accommodation	Yes / No	
Another example showing how arrogance hinders improvement	Yes / No	
A personal experience with being tolerant of someone	Yes / No	
The value of tolerance	Yes / No	
A story of how a famous entrepreneurs tolerates his critics	Yes / No	
The beauty of forgiving	Yes / No	
An example showing how a saint forgives his enemies	Yes / No	
An example showing how someone forgives then regrets	Yes / No	
An example showing how forgiveness is sweetly rewarded	Yes / No	

題目 1.

段落主題	適合嗎？	不可取的原因
The importance of exercise	Yes / **No**	**完全文不對題：** 全篇的主題是cynicism有害健康，這裡卻在談運動。
How cynicism may cause stress	**Yes** / No	
Theories or experiments supporting how cynicism may cause stress	**Yes** / No	
How stress may cause cancer	**Yes** / No	
Statistics showing major causes of cancer	Yes / **No**	**偏離主題：** 雖然前一段提過「緊張可能促成癌症」，但是癌症並非這篇文章的主題，不適合佔用一整段的篇幅。
A fact showing how cynicism affects interpersonal relationships	**Yes** / No	
Wise sayings supporting how appreciation helps avoid cynicism	**Yes** / No	
Experiments or statistics showing appreciative people tend to live longer	**Yes** / No	

題目 2.

段落主題	適合嗎？	不可取的原因
An example showing how humility allows for more accommodation	**Yes** / No	
Another example showing how arrogance hinders improvement	**Yes** / No	
A personal experience with being tolerant of someone	Yes / **No**	偏離主題： 這個只是個人的經驗，和「肚大能容」的整個大格局無關。除非意指自己的經驗證實「肚大能容」，但是即使如此，也並不專業。
The value of tolerance	**Yes** / No	
A story of how a famous entrepreneurs tolerates his critics	**Yes** / No	
The beauty of forgiving	**Yes** / No	
An example showing how a saint forgives his enemies	**Yes** / No	
An example showing how someone forgives then regrets	Yes / **No**	立場不穩： 既然在全文的thesis statement當中，已經表明認同「原諒」的美德，我們就不要節外生枝、自我矛盾。
An example showing how forgiveness is sweetly rewarded	**Yes** / No	

Unit 6

起承轉合（三）
要「轉」得溜

文章之「轉」——Transitions

好文章是一件生動而緊緻的作品,它是一連串的思緒像珍珠一樣連結而成的,環環相扣,一個也不會走樣、更不會鬆掉。然而,當我們的思緒轉換時,文章如何圓潤地發展?例如,我們寫完了某一個觀念之後,該如何順暢地進入另一個觀點?或者,鎖定了某一件事的優點之後,如何順暢地討論它的缺點?為了避免 flow 的突兀,「轉」或「過渡」的角色這時就必須出現了,它就是**轉折語**(用於相異的看法)或**過渡語**(用於同質的看法),英文就是 transitional expressions。

換句話說, transitional expressions 的作用在於**連接**「相異」或「相同」的看法。

有用的 transitions

表達「輕重緩急次序」的轉折語:

1. To start with, (我從頭道來,……)

2. First, second, third, …

3. soon, then, meanwhile, later

4. formerly (前一個)

5. finally (終於)

6. Last but not least, (最後一個重點是……)

7. At first sight, (第一次見面時,……)

8. theoretically (理論上說來,……)

9. hypothetically (假設上說來,……)

10. The priority of… can be shown as follows: (它的優先順序如

下：……）

11. But the... cannot be justified. （但是即使如此，仍有不合理之
    處……）

「順勢」而為的轉折語：

1. similarly （另一個類似的例子是……）

2. furthermore （更進一步地說，……）

3. In conclusion, （結論是……）

4. consequently （因此……）

5. conclusively （總結來說，……）

6. logically （合理地來說，……）

7. more significantly （更重要的是……）

8. unexceptionally （下面這件事，是理所當然的……）

9. unsurprisingly （這是意料之中的事……）

10. supportingly （以下的例子，也將支持前面所說的這個看法……）

11. accordingly （照著這個情況或數字……看來，我們不難猜
    測……）

12. And that is not all. （還有其他類似的狀況，……）

13. But he isn't alone. （除了他以外，還有人也如此……）

14. More examples can be found in... （還有很多例子提供各位參
    考……）

15. But the tragedy didn't end here. （還有更慘的，……）

16. History often repeats itself. （還有類似事件……）

17. The... is echoed with... （事有「迴響」……）

「逆勢」而爲的轉折語：

1. on the contrary （反之，……）

2. to our surprise （沒想到，……）

3. surprisingly （沒想到，……）

4. beyond our imagination （令人感到意外的是，……）

5. Against his own will, … （他並不願意去這麼做，但是……）

6. Strikingly, （令人震驚的一件事是，……）

7. Unfortunately, （不幸地，……）

8. Disasters never occur alone. （真是禍不單行啊！除了前面發生的之外，還有……）

9. But s/he has come a long way. （他很成功，但是他今天的成就得來不易，……）

10. Against all (the) odds, …. （雖然勝算不大，他仍然……）

Transitions 可以自己獨立一段

我在上一章提到，在高級英文作文中，寫作的「邏輯不變、架構可以更靈活！」。怎麼說呢？

所謂「邏輯不變」，就是思緒必然有**始**、有**因**、有**果**、有**終**，也就是「啟、承、轉、合」。所謂「架構可以更靈活」，即如果「轉」的部分夠份量，甚至可**自行獨成一個段落**！

例

題目：An Unforgettable Experience

主文中的某一段：描述在山中迷路的恐懼！

下一段
（由恐懼**轉到**聽到直昇機的欣喜）

這一段因為內容夠
強烈，所以全段獨
立出來，完全做為
上一段和下一段的
transition。

"We're saved!" cried our tour guide on hearing the chopper, whose noisy rotor blades sounded like heavenly music from above.

下一段
（由上直昇機之前的害怕
轉到獲救之後的平安）

大家如何被救上直昇機以及獲救後的心情。

Exercise 7

請嘗試分辨以下的 transition（轉折語）在上下文中是否適合，然後將 **Yes** 或 **No** 圈起。

題目 1.：A Sad Experience

在大 body 中的前一段如下：

Topic Sentence
小 body
Main point: **I've been burdened with apprehension ever since.**　　我自此愁腸百轉

↓

以下的轉折語適合嗎？

Transition: To start with,	適合嗎？Yes / No
Topic Sentence	
小 Body	內容
Main Point	

或

Transition: More examples can be found.	適合嗎？ Yes / No
Topic Sentence	
小 Body	內容
Main Point	

或

Transition: Supportingly, …	適合嗎？ Yes / No
Topic Sentence	
小 Body	內容
Main Point	

或

Transition: Disasters never occur alone.	適合嗎？ Yes / No
Topic Sentence	
小 Body	內容
Main Point	

題目 2.：Child Education

前一段如下：

Topic Sentence
小 body
Main point: **Group activities promote teamwork.** 團體生活確實培養參與團隊的技巧

以下的轉折語適合嗎？

Transition: Supplemental education alone is not enough. 單靠補習教育是不夠的	適合嗎？Yes / No
Topic Sentence	
小 Body	內容
Main Point	

或

Transition: Statistics prove that group activities develop a sense of belonging and understanding. 數據顯示，團體生活可以提昇我們在群體中的歸屬感，並使我們體諒別人	適合嗎？Yes / No
Topic Sentence	
小 Body	內容
Main Point	

或

Transition: Statistically, parents choose courses from a plethora of programs.	適合嗎？Yes / No
Topic Sentence	
小 Body	內容
Main Point	

或

Transition: Statistics strongly support that children who feel comfortable expressing their ideas in a group are better equipped for career success. 數據強烈地證明，能夠在團體中表達想法的孩子，在事業上也較容易成功	適合嗎？Yes / No
Topic Sentence	
小 Body	內容
Main Point	

題目 1.：A Sad Experience

Topic Sentence
小 body
Main point: **I've been burdened with apprehension ever since.**

以下的轉折語適合嗎？

Transition: To start with,	適合嗎？ Yes / No
Topic Sentence	原因：前段的結尾的「愁腸百轉」 ↓如何憂愁？ To start with,（讓我一一數
小 Body	
Main Point	來，……）；接著就可以開始描述了。

或

Transition: More examples can be found.	適合嗎？ Yes / No
Topic Sentence	原因：和前面「愁腸百轉」的意境突 兀，所以這個 linkage 不順暢。
小 Body	
Main Point	

或

Transition: Supportingly, …	適合嗎？ Yes / No
Topic Sentence	原因：“support” 這個字較為嚴肅強硬，意境和上一段的「愁腸百轉」的幽婉也不符，再次顯突兀。
小 Body	
Main Point	

或

Transition: Disasters never occur alone.	適合嗎？ Yes / No
Topic Sentence	原因：前一段是「愁腸百轉」結尾，這一段則表示還有更慘的。在氣勢上順暢地帶出「這一段將更糟」的情景。
小 Body	
Main Point	

題目 2.：Child Education

Topic Sentence
小 body
Main point: **Group activities promote teamwork.**

↓

以下的轉折語適合嗎？

Transition: Supplemental education alone is not enough.	適合嗎？Yes / No
Topic Sentence	原因：前一段的結尾是 group activities（群體生活）和 teamwork （團隊精神）的關係，這裡突然跳到 supplemental education （「補教」，例如 tutoring），破壞 flow，顯得突兀。
小 Body	
Main Point	

或

Transition: Statistics prove that group activities develop a sense of belonging and understanding	適合嗎？Yes / No
Topic Sentence	原因：前一段的結尾是 group activities 和 teamwork 的關係，這一段 transition 提及「數據」如何 support 群體生活的主要性，立刻替這兩個段落先搭起橋樑，而使這兩個段落有順暢有力的 flow。
小 Body	
Main Point	

或

Transition: Statistically, parents choose courses from a plethora of programs. ※ plethora [ˋplɛθərə] (n.) 過多	適合嗎？Yes / No

Topic Sentence	原因：1. 前一段結尾是 group activities 和 teamwork，這一段卻跳到「如何選課程」，顯得突兀。
小 Body	
Main Point	2. 如果把 transition 改成 "To ensure an optimal consequence.（為了確保最好的效益）" 就順暢地連結上一段，並替隨之而來的句子鋪好了路：參與團體生活的最佳態度。

或

Transition: Statistics strongly support that children who feel comfortable expressing their ideas in a group are better equipped for career success.	適合嗎？ Yes / No
Topic Sentence	原因：上一段的結尾是 group activities 和 teamwork，這一段緊接著用數字來支持群體生活的重要性。
小 Body	
Main Point	

Unit 7

起承轉合（四）
水到渠成而「合」

文章之「合」—— Conclusion

任何完整的、有意義的思緒必然有始有終，否則白想一場。寫文章也一樣，有主題，有主文，還有結論。這一部分，在前面已經討論過了。我們這裡僅做個整理。

文章之「合」，就是結論。**結論的宗旨就是回歸全文的主題**，它告訴讀者：

<u>我一開始就這麼說</u>，<u>現在事實證明</u>，<u>我的觀點是正確的</u>！
thesis statement　　　　body　　　　conclusion
（也就是文章的 **theme**）

因此，「結論」就是把「主題」再次強調。

但是為了避免文字疲乏，我們的用字遣詞不能一成不變，須有新氣象才好。結論該怎麼寫留在下一頁再談，我們先看文章必走的路徑。

文章要怎麼「合」

一篇優質英文作文無論在「文字」或是「思緒」方面，從頭到尾，是一個完整的「圓形」。我們用以下的圖形來詮釋，就更清楚了：

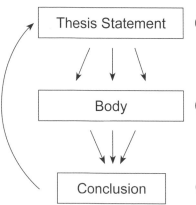

（像馬達一樣，發出力量，打出水流）

（承受了馬達所打出的水流而陸續開花結果）

（收尾，回到 Theme）

我們再進一步認識它們三者之間的關係。

Thesis Statement 和 Body 的關係

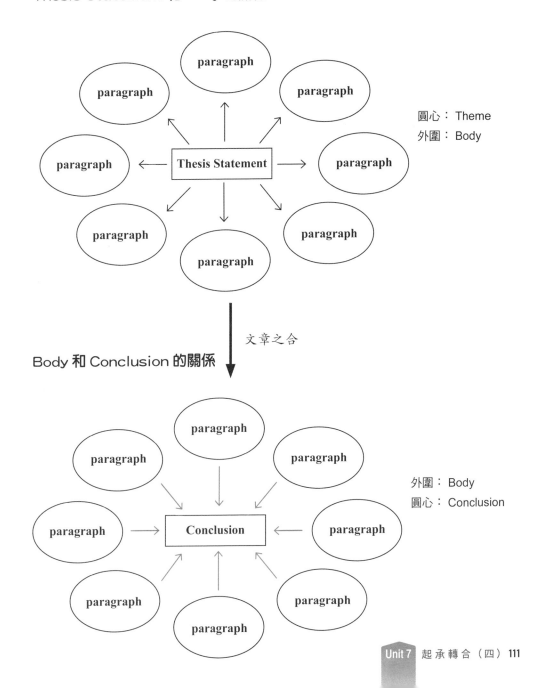

圓心：Theme
外圍：Body

文章之合

Body 和 Conclusion 的關係

外圍：Body
圓心：Conclusion

以上這兩個圖的圓心其實是一模一樣的東西，在一篇優質的英文作文裡面，這兩個圓心的**觀點、內涵、氣勢、意境、形式**完全一樣，只是箭頭的方向不同，以及名稱不同罷了。

> Thesis Statement 和 Conclusion 就像照鏡子，前後同一物。

為了保持連貫，我們就繼續用前面所提的四個最普遍的作文題目，完整地看看一篇英文作文如何寫得快又好。

首先，在高級英文作文中，第一段除了 thesis statement 之外，之前可以再加一個 lead。

Lead + Thesis Statement

我們想像一下：在不遠之處，有一個美麗的花園，外有圍牆，門上有一個小窗，我們可以從窗口望見裡面繽紛燦爛的花朵。英文作文就是要帶領讀者進入這個花園，細細地賞花。那麼，我們如何才能進入這個花園呢？

在英文作文中，lead 就是那一條小徑，把我們帶到門口。Thesis statement 就是那道門，它上面的那扇窗（關鍵字）讓我們得以對花園一窺大概，卻又無法細細欣賞。Body 就是那個美麗的花園，它簇擁了花園裡的各種花朵，讓我們盡情地倘佯在花海之中。Conclusion 就是回到大門，門關上之後了，回頭朝窗內再看一眼。

不過，有的花園有小徑帶路，有的花園則沒有小徑，圍牆就直接呈現在眼前，所以 lead 並非絕對必要。倒是在初級英文作文中，lead 往往免了，因為文字、意境、篇幅未臻成熟，lead 因此使不上勁。

為了多元化練習，以下，我們有時使用 lead，有時則不用 lead，而直接寫 thesis statement。

第一個題目 My Best Friend

文章要「起」了

第一段（Lead + Thesis Statement）

Like a beautiful melody and classic lyrics interweave an intoxicating song,

a great sense of **humor** and loyal **friendship** exemplify my best friend, Tina.

＊前半句是 lead，紅字部分才是真正的 thesis statement。

1. 關鍵字： humor、friendship
2. 主軸與意境： Tina 如同一首美麗的歌曲，令人著迷。

繼續寫，文章要「承」了，
裡面會有好幾個「轉」
（包括「轉折」與「過渡」語）

大 Body

1. 因為每個關鍵字都可以至少寫一段，所以主文至少可以寫兩段。
2. 主文的字數不限、段落不限。數十字至數萬字都可成為佳作。
3. 每一段都鎖定主題，並加以發揮。
4. 每一段都深具內涵。
5. 寫這個題目，一定要融入情感，否則必定失敗。

文章要「合」了

Conclusion

Like a cellist plucks out an enchanting melody that can touch our soul, my

soulmate plays her song with a friendly cheerfulness that enlightens my life.

Conclusion 的主軸和意境巧妙而完整地 echo with the thesis statement：

	全文的第一段 （**Thesis Statement**）	全文的最後一段 （**Conclusion**）
兩者形態一致 （**consistent**） 感覺柔順、不會 頭重腳輕。	一句話 + 真正的 thesis statement	一句話 + 真正的 conclusion
意境與文 **字也一致** （**consistent**）	a beautiful melody　*echoes with*　enchanting melody	
	interweave （織出音樂）　*echoes with*　plucks out （撥彈音樂）	
	humor　*echoes with*　cheerfulness	
	friendship　*echoes with*　friendly	
	an intoxicating song　*echoes with*　soulmate plays her song	

第二個題目 My Mother

文章要「起」了

第一段（Thesis Statement）

（我們這次不用 lead）

The **intelligence** and **altruistic maternal** love of my mother compliments her role as a **housewife**.

1. 關鍵字： intelligence、altruistic、maternal、housewife
2. 主軸與意境：母親雖是家庭主婦，卻兼具睿智與博愛。

繼續寫，文章要「承」了，
裡面會有好幾個「轉」
（包括「轉折」與「過渡」語）

大 Body

1. 每個關鍵字都可以至少寫一段，所以這篇文章的主文至少可以寫四段。
2. 字數不限、段落不限。數十字至數萬字都可能成佳作。
3. 每一段都鎖定主題，並加以發揮。
4. 每一段都深具內涵。
5. 寫這個題目，也一定要融入情感，否則必定失敗。

文章要「合」了

Conclusion

I'm bestowed with a seemingly common yet most extraordinary mother who exemplifies the value of true wisdom and unselfish love.

Conclusion 的主軸與意境巧妙而完整地 echo with the thesis statement：

	全文的第一段 （**Thesis Statement**）	全文的最後一段 （**Conclusion**）
兩者形態 **consistent**	只有 thesis statement， 沒有另加 lead	只有 conclusion， 沒有另加 supplement
意境與文字也 **consistent**	intelligence　　*echoes with*	true wisdom
	altruistic　　*echoes with*	unselfish
	maternal love　　*echoes with*	mother; love
	housewife　　*echoes with*	common mother

第三個題目 On Mixed-Cultural Marriages

文章要「起」了

第一段（Lead + Thesis Statement）

這一次示範使用 lead，紅字部分才是真正的主軸。

Like chocolate chips in ice cream or a square peg in a round hole, a mixed-cultural marriage can be **flavorful** yet unavoidably faces **conflicts**, ranging from **cuisine** to **family values**.

1. Lead 使用的諺語 "A and B are like a square peg in a round hole." 意思是「格格不入」。
2. 關鍵字： flavorful、conflicts、cuisine、family value(s)

繼續寫，文章要「承」了，
裡面會有好幾個「轉」
（包括「轉折」與「過渡」語）

大 Body

1. 每個關鍵字都可以至少寫一段，所以這一篇文章的主文至少可寫四段。
2. 字數不限、段落不限。數十字至數萬字都可能成佳作。
3. 每一段都鎖定主題，並加以發揮。
4. 每一段都深具內涵。
5. 這個題目可加入情感，而成為一篇抒情文，也可以純論述而成為論說文，亦可兩者兼具，展現剛柔並濟的綜合文體。

文章要「合」了

Conclusion

As "the die is already cast," wontons and clam chowder can be equally delicious, and both core and extended family are equally valuable.

> 1. 關鍵字： delicious、family、valuable
>
> 2. 也使用了諺語 "the die is already cast" ，意思是「木已成舟」。

Conclusion 的主軸與意境巧妙而完整地 echo with the thesis statement：

	全文的第一段 （Thesis Statement）	全文的最後一段 （Conclusion）
兩者形態 **consistent**	一句話 + thesis statement	一句話 + conclusion
意境與文字也 **consistent**	引用諺語： "Like a square peg in a round hole. *echoes with*	引用諺語： "the die is already cast"
	cuisine *echoes with*	wontons and clam chowder
	family values *echoes with*	core and extended family

※ core family 小家庭； extended family 大家庭

第四個題目 My Definition of Beauty

文章要「起」了

第一段（Thesis Statement）

我們這一次不用 lead

Genuine **generosity**, true **mercifulness**, and unchallengeable **wisdom** accent the charisma of the **old age**—the image of real beauty.

1. 關鍵字： generosity、mercifulness、wisdom、old age
2. 主軸與意境：感性與理性兼具。 "generous、merciful、beautiful" 是偏感性的描述；同時 "generosity、wisdom、image" 則是偏理性的產物。 （※ generosity 既理性又感性）

繼續寫，文章要「承」了，
裡面會有好幾個「轉」
（包括「轉折」與「過渡」語）

大 Body

1. 每一個關鍵字至少可以寫一段，所以這一篇文章的主文至少可寫四段。
2. 短至數段、長至數萬段皆可。
3. 每一段都鎖定主軸（the beauty of the old age）。
4. 深具內涵。
5. 寫這個題目須情感與評論兼具，才同時展現理性和感性。

文章要「合」了

Conclusion

A portrait of an old gentleman whose eyes beam the glow of **generosity, tender-heartedness**, and **wisdom** would be a most **beautiful** piece of art about human life.

1. 關鍵字： generosity、tender-heartedness、wisdom、beautiful
2. 意境：兼具情感性與評論。
   感性： portrait、generosity、tender-heartedness、art piece
   理性： generosity、wisdom

Conclusion 的主軸與意境巧妙而完整地 echo with the thesis statement：

	全文的第一段 （Thesis Statement）	全文的最後一段 （Conclusion）
兩者形態 consistent	只有一個簡單句	只有一個簡單句
意境與文字也 consistent	genuine generosity　*echoes with*	(beam the glow of) generosity
	true mercifulness　*echoes with*	(beam the glow of) tender-heartedness
	unchallengeable wisdom　*echoes with*	(beam the glow of) wisdom
	real beauty　*echoes with*	piece of art

　　所以，英文作文真的不難寫，只要隨著「起、承、轉、合」這個邏輯，就不會偏離主題，而且創造圓順的 flow ；也因為成功地鎖定了主題，而愈走愈深入，自然而然展現了綿密而邏輯的思考，最後自然水到渠成，成就了令人信服的結論。

　　總之，從一下筆開始，就繞著 thesis statement，完整地鎖住主題，使 main idea 如影隨形，經由 body 的 powerful 卻 exquisite 的發揮，再產

生了 conclusion，也就是把讀者帶回到文章一開始就主張的觀點。

　　好的文章必有極高的可信度和說服力，即使我們的讀者或許意見相左（例如論說文可能遭遇讀者持有不同的意見），但是因為文章的邏輯堅固、文筆優美、思緒細膩、數字和例子具有相當的說服力，作者的專業和努力必使文章不同凡響。

Exercise 8

請先看完以下的題目， 再看以下每一題的 conclusion 是否完全搭配 thesis statement 和 body。

1. 作文題目 ： On Negotiating

「起」

Thesis Statement

Negotiating is an essential "give and take" skill to reach mutually acceptable agreements with colleagues, spouses, and even children.

「談判」是一種很有用的技巧，它包括了「給」與「取」，可以幫助我們和同事、配偶甚至孩子取得雙方皆認可的協議。

要「承」了

First Paragraph

主題： the definition of negotiation

+

更多 Paragraphs

主題： the techniques of negotiation

這一部份可以有許多段落，例如：

1. Prepare the desired settlement point （準備心中的目標）至少一段
2. Identify the needs of the other side （了解對方的需要）至少一段
3. Ask questions （要會提問）至少一段
4. Listen （要會傾聽）至少一段
5. Stay issue oriented （不要被對方模糊焦點）至少一段

6. Control emotions （情緒要穩定）至少一段

7. Make concessions （要懂得讓步）至少一段

etc.

+

如果要寫更多 Paragraphs

舉例證明 the importance of negotiating

和 colleagues 的溝通至少一段

和 spouse 的溝通至少一段

和 children 的溝通至少一段

↓ 文章要「合」了

以下請作答：

這個結論好嗎？ Yes / No

Conclusion A

To sum up, negotiation plays a vital role in our lives, which is a job we must not ignore.

這個結論好嗎？ Yes / No

Conclusion B

Negotiation requires considerable effort, but the reward is definitely sweet!

這個結論好嗎？ Yes / No

Conclusion C
Collaborative negotiations, a process of exchange, get our needs met while preserving cordial interpersonal relationships.

2. 作文題目 ： Advantages of Jogging

「起」

Thesis Statement
Jogging conditions the heart and lungs, improves muscle tone and strength, and relieves pressure and stress—and just about anyone at any age can do it! 「慢跑」可以調節我們的心臟和肺臟，促進肌肉的訓練、提昇肌力，而且還可以舒壓。最重要的是，這是不分年齡的運動！

要「承」了

Body
1. conditions the heart 至少一段（若多寫長一點，也可以「原因」寫一段、「例子」寫一段、「數據」寫一段）
2. improves muscle tone and strength 至少一段（也可同上面，寫好幾段）
3. relieves pressure and stress 至少一段（也可同上一段一樣，寫好幾段）

文章要「合」了

以下請作答 ：

這個結論好嗎？ Yes / No

Conclusion A
Jogging is indeed an effective form of exercise, even though it may result in joint problems.

這個結論好嗎？ Yes / No

Conclusion B
Just a good pair of running shoes can bring us effective and efficient cardiovascular, muscular, and bone fitness. Imagine the possibilites!

這個結論好嗎？ Yes / No

Conclusion C
If we wish to burn calories or prevent heart disease, jogging regularly is an excellent choice.

參考答案

1.

這個結論好嗎？ Yes / **No**

Conclusion A
To sum up, negotiation plays a vital role in our lives and is a job we must not ignore.
原因： 1. 思想空淺、文字也太隨便。 2. 自說自話，腦中沒有一致性，也沒有 echo the thesis statement。

這個結論好嗎？ Yes / **No**

Conclusion B
Negotiation requires considerable effort, but the reward is definitely sweet!
原因： 1. 這只是全文當中某一個小論點的結論（例如「談判」是辛苦的）， 　份量不夠做全文的結論。 2. 未能 echo thesis statement。

這個結論好嗎？ **Yes** / No

Conclusion C
Collaborative negotiations, a process of exchange, get our needs met while preserving cordial interpersonal relationships.

原因：主軸、文字和意境均靈巧而完整地 echo the thesis statement。		
thesis statement		**conclusion**
give and take	*echoes with*	process of exchange
mutually acceptable	*echoes with*	cordial interpersonal relationships
colleges, spouse, children	*echoes with*	interpersonal

2.

這個結論好嗎？ Yes / **No**

Conclusion A
Jogging is indeed an effective form of exercise, even though it may result in joint problems.
原因：在 thesis statement 中提及 jogging 的優點，結論卻提到 jogging 有傷關節。如此結尾，顯得腦筋錯亂。

這個結論好嗎？ **Yes** / No

Conclusion B		
Just a good pair of running shoes can bring us effective and efficient cardiovascular, muscular, and bone fitness. Imagine the possibilites!		
原因：主軸、意境和文字均靈巧而完整 echo the thesis statement。		
thesis statement		**conclusion**
heart and lungs	*echoes with*	cardiovascular
muscle tone and strength	*echoes with*	muscular and bone fitness

這個結論好嗎？ Yes / **No**

Conclusion C
If we wish to burn calories or prevent heart disease, jogging regularly is an excellent choice.
原因：並未完全 echo the thesis statement，顯得寫作的思緒不夠完整、也不細膩。

Unit **8**

內涵決定深度

我們從小就會哼哼唱唱「一閃一閃小星星」，它的曲調活潑、旋律優美、伴隨著我們的童年。但是經由莫札特寫成「小星星變奏曲」之後，主旋律依舊，內涵則因為十分地豐富，所以意境迥然不同，成為一首細緻、龐大、迷人的、被許多鋼琴大師演奏過的鋼琴曲。

我們常看到蓋房子，在同樣的地區，用同樣的價錢，同樣的時間，有些人蓋得平凡通俗，並不特別引人注意；有些人則可蓋出精巧脫俗的藝術品。

寫作也完全一樣，同一個題目，有些人寫得幼稚，令人搖頭；有些人寫得平庸，讓人過目即忘；有些人則寫出深具內涵，令人讚賞的文章，三者的層次差距當然很大。

既然內涵如此重要，我們的作文焉能沒有它？那麼，內涵由何而來呢？我們如何去創造它呢？為了方便各位讀者學習，我把英文寫作的內涵分為**主觀**和**客觀**兩種：

主觀方面的 Input：

1. 個人的經驗：少則一段，多則不限。
2. 個人對別人的觀察：少則一段，多則不限。
3. 個人的看法和感動（這個比較狹隘，因為它完全來自個人）：少則一段，多則不限。

缺乏內涵是我們讀者寫英文作文的致命傷。我常替報社以及大學盃英文作文比賽服務，發現大部分的作品均偏向「主觀性」，使內涵因此欠缺深度和廣度。

寫英文作文絕對不可純主觀！人都是有限的，再聰明的人，思考必仍

有所不足；再有知識的人，資訊必仍有所不足；再具人生經驗的人，經歷必仍有所不足。一篇好的作品，必須呈現廣度和深度，如果僅靠主觀方面的支柱，會呈現一面倒的單薄。

客觀方面的 Input：

這個可就豐富了，因為它走出了我們自己的世界，進入了所謂 "The sky is the only limit." 的格局，使文章立刻脫胎換骨。

客觀的 input 包括：

1. **例子**：在社會中，相關的例子太多了，我們在擷取例子的時候以愈出名的愈好。例如，要談到「愛」，與其舉自己的父母為例，就不如以 Mother Teresa 或證嚴法師為例。

2. **數據**：數據來自**研究**，**新聞刊物**、**書本**、**期刊**、**網路**皆可提供豐富的數據。

3. **網路**：網路是高級英文作文寫作的好幫手，它有各式各樣的資訊。

4. **實人實地採訪**：Interview 的對象不限，可以是平凡人，也可以是文章的主角或有關的專家，只要他們言之有物，就可放入主文。

5. **書籍**：書籍是作者的智慧結晶，很有貢獻。

6. **論文**（它尤其提供豐富的數據）：論文是作者多方考證和研究的成果，有許多專業知識，可以使作文更顯專業。

7. **詩詞**：詩詞橫跨古今而不墜，又是藝術的結晶，自有它迷人之處。

8. **歷史**：歷史是一面鏡子，也是歲月的聚寶盒，有絕對的說服力。

9. **別人的智慧之語**：自己不夠智慧，若是借用別人的智慧之語來支持我們的文章，也是智慧！

讀者想一想，文章的內涵是不是很容易就建立起來了呢？而且，愈長

的文章，段落愈多、深度與廣度愈多，自然而然地應該更具內涵，而不是時常聽到的訴苦：「要寫那麼多字！怎麼寫？」 有了以上主觀和客觀的 input，我們可以確信英文寫作真的輕鬆！短文長文都簡單！只要方法對了，何必搔破白頭呢？

接下來，請先看以下的範文。後面會有更清楚的說明。

The Beauty of Chinese Literature

A Chinese poet once said, "Artistic talent displays the landscape of the human heart, and landscapes are an artistic gift from Mother Nature."[1] Indeed the exquisite artistry and intertwined sentiments of Chinese poetry have penetrated Chinese culture for centuries.

Some poetry simply admires the beauty of nature:

Birds fly into the sunset glow;
And rivers inlay the horizons aglow.[2]

「落霞與孤鶩齊飛，
秋水共長天一色。」 ——唐・王渤

This 1,425-year-old poem reveals the beauty of nature in two extremes. First it focuses on the beauty of nature in motion. Next it shows the beauty of nature in a static state. A dynamic image is contrasted with a static one; birds gracefully flying into a hazy sunset versus a sleepy river reflecting the last light of the day. Both evoke a sense of natural beauty tied together by the setting Sun's waning glow.

Some poetry is metaphorical:

Beanstalks fervently burn to heat the fire;
On the fire are beans in the pot.
Beans utter sad calls,
"You and I were once one,
Please spare some mercy for me!"[3]

「煮豆燃豆萁，
豆在斧中泣：
本是同根生，
相煎何太急！」──東漢‧曹植

This 1,882-year-old poem is known as the Seven Pace Poem. In the late Eastern-Han Dynasty (circa AD 220), the king-to-be Cao Pi schemed to kill his extremely intelligent brother, Cao Zhi, by ordering him to compose a poem within seven paces. This is the poem that Cao Zhi came up with. It is particularly piercing because it is a metaphor for the relationship with his brother. The beanstalks and beans both come from one plant. They are one and the same, yet the beanstalks work fervently to heat the fire that burns the beans. It is a touching plea for mercy from one who has been wronged by his own kin.

A poem even changed Chinese history.

Gloriously, the sunset glows;[4]
But the nightfall is close.

「夕陽無限好，
只是近黃昏。」——清・李商隱

This 1,266-year-old poem originally addressed human mortality and played on a deep sentimental attachment to life, but was appropriated by former Chinese leader Deng Xiaoping when his reform plan was boycotted by conservative political power-holders. Deng used the sentiments of past glory and loss that were already associated with this poem and transferred them to a patriotic context. He referred to the old, glorious China which had long been behind the bamboo curtain and which would soon meet the nightfall brought about by globalization and global competition. The only way to bring China back to glory was to adapt and reform. The indisputable truth of his message was heard by millions and quieted the opposition, removing the obstacles to reform and making China what it is today.

As in many poetic traditions, numerous Chinese poems are about love. The following contains a theme that has stricken many souls over the centuries:

Silkworms only die after the last mouthful of silk is spun;

Candle tears only dry after the last inch of wick is burned.[5]

「春蠶到死絲方盡，

蠟炬成灰淚始乾。」——李商隱

This 1,266-year-old poem talks of the sacrificial love of parents and lovers. Countless romantic stories have powerfully illustrated such love. As an example, for Christians, love is best exemplified by the sacrifice of Jesus on the cross, who shed his last drop of blood for the sins of all humanity.

The place of poetry in Chinese history is irreplaceable. Not only do poems tell of the times in which they were created, but they also speak of things that are timeless and universal: love and loss; wisdom and art. Chinese culture is intertwined with its poetry, which can not only touch the heartstrings, but influence an entire nation.

---

1. Li Yu, Qing Dynasty (1644-1911) poet.

2. Wang Bao, Tang Dynasty (618-907) poet.

3. Cao Zhi, late Eastern-Han Dynasty (25-220) poet.

4. Li Shangyin, Qing Dynasty poet.

5. Li Shangyin.

下一頁起，我們將文章的結構標示出來，提供讀者作為對照。

The Beauty of Chinese Literature

↓ 開始 「起」

(lead ▶) A Chinese poet once said, "Artistic talent displays the landscape of the human heart, and landscapes are an artistic gift from Mother Nature." (Thesis Statement ▶) **Indeed the exquisite artistry and intertwined sentiments of Chinese poetry have penetrated Chinese culture for centuries.**

↓ 開始 「承」

Some poetry simply admires the beauty of nature:

Birds fly into the sunset glow;
And rivers inlay the horizons aglow.

轉折語 ①

大 Body
開始：
例一

「落霞與孤鶩齊飛，

秋水共長天一色。」 ——唐‧王渤

(topic sentence ▶) **This 1,425-year-old poem reveals the beauty of nature in two extremes.** (小body ▶) First it focuses on the beauty of nature in motion. Next it shows the beauty of nature in a static state. A dynamic image is contrasted with a static one; birds gracefully flying into a hazy sunset versus a sleepy river reflecting the last light of the day. (viewpoint ▶) **Both evoke a sense of natural beauty tied together the setting Sun's waning glow.**

Some poetry is metaphorical:

Beanstalks fervently burn to heat the fire;
On the fire are beans in the pot.
Beans utter sad calls,
'You and I were once one,
Please spare some mercy for me!

轉折語 ②

「煮豆燃豆萁，
豆在斧中泣：
本是同根生，
相煎何太急！」——東漢 · 曹植

例二

(topic sentence ▶) **This 1,882-year-old poem is known as the Seven Pace Poem.** (小body ▶) In the late Eastern-Han Dynasty (circa AD 220), the king-to-be Cao Pi schemed to kill his extremely intelligent brother, Cao Zhi, by ordering him to compose a poem within seven paces. This is the poem that Cao Zhi came up with. It is particularly piercing because it is a metaphor for the relationship with his brother. The beanstalks and beans both come from one plant. They are one and the same, yet the beanstalks work fervently to heat the fire that burns the beans. (viewpoint ▶) **<u>It is a touching plea for mercy from one who has been wronged by his own kin.</u>**

A poem even changed Chinese history:

> *Gloriously, the sunset glows;*
> *But the nightfall is close.*
>
> 「夕陽無限好，
> 只是近黃昏。」——清‧李商隱

轉折語 ③

(topic sentence ▶) **This 1,266-year-old poem originally addressed human mortality and played on a deep sentimental attachment to life, but was appropriated by former Chinese leader Deng Xiaoping when his reform plan was boycotted by conservative political power-holders.** (小body ▶) Deng used the sentiments of past glory and loss that were already associated with this poem and transferred them to a patriotic context. He referred to the old, glorious China which had long been behind the bamboo curtain and which would soon meet the "nightfall" brought about by globalization and global competition. The only way to bring China back to glory was to adapt and reform. (viewpoint ▶) <u>**The indisputable truth of his message was heard by millions and quieted the opposition, removing the obstacles to reform and making China what it is today.**</u>

例三

As in many poetic traditions, numerous Chinese poems are about love. The following contains a theme that has stricken many souls over the centuries:

Silkworms only die after the last mouthful of silk is spun;
Candle tears only dry after the last inch of wick is burned.

「春蠶到死絲方盡，
蠟炬成灰淚始乾。」——李商隱

例四

(topic sentence ▶) **This 1,266-year-old poem talks of the sacrificial love of parents and lovers.** (小body ▶) Countless romantic stories have powerfully illustrated such love. (viewpoint ▶) **As an example, for Christians, love is best exemplified by the sacrifice of Jesus on the cross, who shed his last drop of blood for the sins of all humanity.**

↓ 開始 「合」

The place of poetry in Chinese history is undeniable. Not only do poems tell of the times in which they were created, but they also speak of things that are timeless and universal: love and loss; wisdom and art. Chinese culture is intertwined with its poetry, which can not only touch the heartstrings, but also influence an entire nation.

結論

Unit 9

細膩的文字帶來感動

粗枝大葉的丈夫，常令妻子不安；細心體貼的丈夫，則讓妻子感到溫暖。生澀粗嘎的音樂，常令人心神難寧；細緻典雅的音樂，則令人陶醉。

英文作文完全一樣，細膩貼切的文筆立刻為作品帶來令人樂於細細品味的質感。

 ## 細膩的文筆從何而來？

其實在寫英文作文時，只要做到以下幾點，每一個人都可以擁有絕佳的文筆：

1. 字彙要細膩精巧

前面已經舉出英文作文最常見到的慣用語，我們隨後將立刻更進一步，直接用替換法，示範如何讓我們的字彙變得更精緻巧妙。

2. 寫作要有感情

不帶感情而寫出的歌曲，難以感動人；不帶感情而演出的電影，也難以感動人。寫作何能例外？文章就像是一場演說、甚至是一篇告白，它和讀者應當有濃郁的心靈溝通。不用感情而寫出的文章，連自己都不覺感動，又如何能夠撥動別人的心靈之弦呢？

3. 思想要純正

一個長相美麗、打扮精緻的女孩，如果沒有一個高貴的靈魂，就不會吸引人。同樣地，再優美的字彙詞藻，再細膩的感情，如果思想不正（例如怨天尤人、傳達不道德的看法、自私、狹隘、抄襲），就絕對無法展現令人如沐春風的氣質，寫了還不如不寫！

以下僅提供數例，讀者總是要多讀書，吸取更多優美的字彙，只要努力，每一位讀者都做得到。給各位一個鼓勵：我的學生必須在半秒鐘之內，立刻流暢地「口說」以下文字的轉換。

 換成高手用字 1 —形容詞：

中文	初級英文常使用	可以換成這個常用字
清楚的	clear	explicit [ɪk`splɪsɪt]
多話的	talkative	loquacious [lo`kweʃəs]
		bombastic
好運的	lucky	blessed
		fortunate
不好的	bad	negative
		odious [`odɪəs]
		abominable [ə`bɑmənəbl̩] 例 abominable behavior就常在寫作中使用
光亮的	bright	brilliant
		luminous [`lumənəs]

廣闊的	broad	extensive
		wide-ranging
		widespread
好管閒事的	nosy	meddlesome [ˋmɛdl̩səm]
		officious [əˋfɪʃəs]
公然的;公開的	open	undisguised [ˌʌndɪsˋgaɪzd]
		thinly-veiled
精緻的	fine	exquisite [ˋɛkskwɪzɪt]
		intricate [ˋɪntrəkɪt]
害羞的	shy	bashful
震驚的	shocked	astonished
		stunned
		thrilled
堅硬的	hard	stiff（硬實的）
		fortified
		rigid [ˋrɪdʒɪd]（僵硬的）
		solid（紮實的）

柔軟的	soft	mild（溫和的）
		supple [`sʌpl]（柔情的；唯唯諾諾的）
		pliable [`plaɪəbl]（易折的；順從的）
微弱的	weak	feeble
		fragile [`frædʒəl]
詳細的	detailed	minute [maɪ`njut]
		particular
		elaborate
確定的	true; assured	definite
		conclusive
		irrefutable
		absolute
有限的	limited	confined
		finite [`faɪnaɪt]

重要的	important	crucial
		essential
		imperative [ɪm`pɛrətɪv]（絕對重要）
		significant
很棒的	wonderful; excellent	marvelous
		ingenious [ɪn`dʒinjəs]
		remarkable
快樂的	happy	cheerful
		elated [ɪ`letɪd]
		joyful
過時的	old-fashioned	outdated
		out-of-date
		obsolete [`ɑbsə͵lit]
		outmoded
富裕的	rich	wealthy
		affluent [`æfluənt]

貧窮的	poor	shanty [`ʃæntɪ]
		scanty [`skæntɪ]
可憐的	poor	miserable
		wretched [`rɛtʃɪd]
		pathetic
		pitiful
示範性的	showing	exemplary [ɪg`zɛmplərɪ]
		demonstrating
瘋狂的	crazy	insane（指精神方面）
		frenetic [frɪ`nɛtɪk]（指交易、宗教）
		radical（激進的）
憤怒的	angry	furious [`fjʊrɪəs]
		irritated（被惹怒的）
關鍵的	key	crucial
		critical
		decisive [dɪ`saɪsɪv]

卑鄙的	mean	despicable [ˋdɛspɪkəbl]
		base
		comtemptible
有害的	harmful	detrimental [ˏdɛtrəˋmɛntl]
		devastating [ˋdɛvəsˏtetɪŋ]（害處極大的、具毀滅性的）
		disastrous [dɪzˋæstrəs]
		traumatic [trɔˋmætɪk]（會帶來創傷的）
		pernicious [pəˋnɪʃəs]（很有害的）
		catastrophic [ˏkætəˋstrafɪk]（天災方面）
有助的	helpful	valuable
		conducive
		advantageous [ædˋvəntedʒəs]
		beneficial
		favourable
天生的	born	congenital [kənˋdʒɛnətl]
		hereditary [həˋrɛdəˏtɛrɪ]（遺傳的）

大膽的	bold	audacious [ɔ`deʃəs]
		daring
聰明的	smart bright	intelligent
		clever
		astute [ə`stjut]（機靈的）
		resourceful（思想很快的）
		shrewd（精明的）
完美的	perfect	flawless
		impeccable [ɪm`pɛkəbl̩]
簡單扼要的	brief	concise [kən`saɪs]
		succinct [sək`sɪŋkt]
根本的	basic	elemantary（初步的）
		primary（根本而主要的）
		fundamental（基礎所需的）
		underlying（根本且十分重要的）
粗俗的	rude	vulgar [`vʌlgə]
		uncivilized

真的	real; true	actual（事實如此的）
		genuine [`dʒɛnjuɪn]（純正的）
		authentic [ɔ`θɛntɪk]（十分逼真的）
假的	fake	phony [`fonɪ]
		pseudo [`sudo]（冒牌、冒名的）
小心謹慎的	careful	prudent
		provident [`prɑvədənt]（深謀遠慮的）
務實的	practical	pragmatic
盛行的	popular	prevalent [`prɛvələnt]
		widespread
		faddish [`fædɪʃ]（成為風尚的）
美麗的；迷人的	beautiful; charming	picturesque [ˌpɪktʃə`rɛsk]（美如畫的）
		glamorous [`glæmərəs]
		breath-taking
		stunning
		charismatic [ˌkærɪz`mætɪk]（有魅力的）

逼真的	real	lifelike
		authentic [ɔ`θɛntɪk]
冷淡的	cold	remote
		detached [dɪ`tætʃt]
有名的	famous	prestigious [prɛs`tɪdʒɪəs]
		illustrious [ɪ`lʌstrɪəs]
		reputable [`rɛpjətəbl]
即將來臨的	coming	upcoming
		impending
		approaching
		imminent [`ɪmənənt]（迫在眉睫的）
可疑的	suspicious	skeptical
		dubious

請替換以下畫線部分的文字

1. a <u>clear</u> voice → _____

2. <u>bad</u> behavior → _____

3. <u>nosy</u> → _____

4. <u>soft</u> character → _____

5. a <u>detailed</u> description → _____

6. <u>important</u> → _____

7. a <u>mean</u> idea → _____

8. a <u>perfect</u> design → _____

9. a <u>fake</u> name → _____

10. a <u>coming</u> storm → _____

1. (an) explicit

2. abominable

3. meddlesome

4. supple

5. elaborated

6. crucial

7. despicable

8. (an) impeccable

9. phony

10. (an) approaching

換成高手用字 2 —善用複合形容詞（Compound Adjectives）

　　形容詞在用字遣詞上佔極重要的地位。其實，除了單字之外，複合字也是非常有力的形容詞。以下是很實用的複合形容詞，讀者要記背起來。

涵蓋範圍很廣的	wide-ranging 例 The plague, which covers a wide area, has killed 220 people. 　　↓ 改為 The **wide-ranging** plague has caused 220 fatalities. <div align="right">[fə`tælətɪ]</div>
全國的	nation-wide 例 These contests are conducted throughout the whole country, and many people are participating. 　　↓ 改為 These **nation-wide** contests have drawn numerous participants.
解決麻煩的	trouble-shooting 例 He always knows how to solve problems. 　　↓ 改為 He is good at **trouble-shooting**. （或 He is a good troubleshooter.）

破紀錄的	record-breaking 例 His speed has broken the record. It only took him three minutes to complete the event. ↓ 改為 His **record-breaking** speed was three minutes.
高調的	high-profile 例 Her high position in the government draws a lot of public attention. ↓ 改為 She has a **high-profile** government position.
低調的	low-profile 例 In order to protect yourself, try not to draw too much attention to yourself. ↓ 改為 Keeping your actions **low-profile** is a good idea.
職位高的	high-ranking 例 He has a very high position in the government. ↓ 改為 He is a **high-ranking** official.
全面性的	across-the-board; full-scale 例 Please prepare this completely. ↓ 改為 Please make **full-scale** preparations.

危機重重的	crisis-ridden 　　　[1] 例 The country is faced with many crises. 　　↓ 改為 The country is **crisis-ridden**.
飽受戰爭之害的	war-ridden 例 The Middle East has long suffered from wars. 　　↓ 改為 The Middle East is **war-ridden**.
債台高築的	debt-ridden 例 He owes people a lot of money. 　　↓ 改為 He is heavily **debt-ridden**.
是非分明的； 寫得清清楚楚的	black-and-white 例 What can and can't be done is written very clearly. 　　↓ 改為 The musts and mustn'ts are written in <u>**black and white**</u>. 　　　　　　　　　　（名詞，中間不加 hyphen）
久被擱置的	long-stalled 例 He has delayed this proposal, which should be turned in tomorrow. 　　↓ 改為 This **long-stalled** proposal is due tomorrow.

以家庭為重的	family-oriented 　　　[`orɪɛntɪd] 例 In my sister's heart, nothing is more important than her family. 　　↓ 改為 My sister is **family-oriented**.
以事業為重的	career-oriented 例 John does everything for his career. 　　↓ 改為 John is **career-oriented**.
人口稀少的 （國家或地區）	sparsely-populated 例 Even though there aren't many people in the country, all of them look very happy. 　　↓ 改為 People in this **sparsely-populated** country seem content.
人口眾多的	heavily-populated 例 There are so many people living in India; meanwhile, India is becoming prosperous. 　　↓ 改為 **Heavily-populated** India is prospering.

彌補缺失的	fence-mending 例 We need several methods to solve this problem. 　　↓ 改為 Several **fence-mending** measures are required.
填鴨式的	force-fed 例 If students learn in a forced way, they will not be able to think creatively. 　　↓ 改為 **Forced-fed** education deprives students of their originality.

Exercise 10

請使用複合形容詞以及比較細緻的文字，重寫以下句子。

1. Economists are trying very hard to face the global financial storm.

答案：_____

2. It's not good if parents force their children to learn things.

答案：_____

3. Because of the small population, Canada welcomes people to immigrate there.

答案：_____

4. All husbands and wives should make the family first priority.

答案：_____

5. This country has so many crises that it may go bankrupt soon.

答案：_____

6. He does only things right and hates to be wrong.

答案：_____

7. We already stated the rules very clearly in the contract, and we should follow them.

答案：_____

8. China had so many wars during the Spring and Autumn Period (270-476 BC) that many suffered from hunger.

答案：_____

9. He works for the company, and his position is very high.

答案：_____

10. Even though he is very successful, he still remains humble and keeps to himself.

答案：_____

（以下答案只是參考，讀者可由書本中找出更多的進階用法）

1. Economists strive for fence-mending measures during the global financial storm.

2. Force-fed education isn't recommended.

3. Sparsely-populated Canada recruits emigrants worldwide.

4. The married should be family-oriented.

5. This crisis-ridden company is faced with imminent bankruptcy.

6. He believes in keeping things black and white.

7. This black-and-white contract should be respected.

8. Hunger prevailed in the war-ridden Spring and Autumn Period of China.

（※在高級英文寫作中，各種資料都需嚴謹，才有credibility。因此，「春秋時期」在英文作文中不可單獨出現，而需立即補上年代。）

9. He is a high-ranking employee in the company.

10. He is very low-profile about his success.

換成高手用字 3 —動詞

我常說動詞是句子的靈魂，絕對不可隨便使用。以下是英文作文經常需要用到的意涵，我們將這些英文進階。

中文	常使用	除此之外，還有
問	ask	inquire
回溯	look back	resound（一邊追憶，一邊說出來）
		recall
花費	cost	consume
恨	hate	loathe [loð]
		detest
改變	change	shift 例：shift one's ground（轉變立場）
		transform（大轉變、脫胎換骨）
		alter
抓住	catch; hold	grip
		grab
		grasp
		seize

注視	look	gaze
		behold
監督	monitor	oversee
		supervise
		superintend
想像	imagine	fancy
		visualize [`vɪʒʊəˌlaɪz]
限制	limit	confine
		restrict
動	move	undulate [`ʌndjəˌlet]（一波波移動，例如稻田）
		fluctuate [`flʌktʃuˌet]（上下波動；例如股市）
加強、強調	strengthen; emphasize	enhance
		intensify
		heighten
		augment
		reinforce [ˌriɪn`fɔrs]

淡化	play... down	dilute [daɪ`lut]
舉行	hold	put on
		conduct
		stage
		host（舉辦宴會）
警告	warn	exhort [ɪg`zɔrt]
告訴	tell	notify [`notə͵faɪ]
		inform
丟臉	lose face	be disgraced be embarrassed
抵抗	fight against	confront
		resist（主動地抗拒） 例：resist temptations
		withstand（被動地抗拒；奮力站穩地抵擋） 例：withstand natural calamities [kə`læmətɪ]
		rebound（反彈）

加速進行；促成	speed up	accelerate [æk`sɛləˌrət]
		facilitate [fə`sɪləˌtet]
避免	avoid	shun [ʃʌn]
		avert [ə`vɜt]
罵	scold; blame	rebuke
		condemn
		chide [tʃaɪd]
講述	talk about	depict
		broach [brotʃ]（開始講述）
		recount（限定講述已發生之事）
		delineate [dɪ`lɪnɪˌet]（描出輪廓）
		elaborate（詳述）
		portray（細細地描述）
修正	correct	redress
		amend
		rectify [`rɛktəˌfaɪ]
實現	come true	materialize [mə`tɪrɪəˌlaɪz]
		realize

停止	stop	halt
		cease
		pause
妨礙	hinder	hamper
		impede [ɪm`pid]
令人害怕	scare	intimidate
		frighten
		petrify
		terrify
超越	pass	overwhelm
		overshadow（令別人遜色）
對……有害	harm	plague [pleg]
		injure
跌落	fall	tumble（亦指心情、股價……）
應付	handle	manage
		tackle [`tækl]
交出	turn in	submit

預見	predict	foresee
		envision [ɪn`vɪʒən]
支持	support back up	bolster（有聲援之意）
		buttress
增加	increase add	intensify
		boost（快速增加）
		raise
		augment
		multiply
減少	decrease	dwindle [`dwɪndl̩]
		dilute [daɪ`lut]
		curtail（削減）
		alleviate [ə`livɪet]（減輕）
		downsize（減少規模）
確定	assure	confirm
		define
		affirm
		acknowledge

假設	suppose	assume
		presume
		hypothesize [haɪ`pɑθəsaɪz]
破壞	break	mar
		wreck
		sabotage [`sæbəˌtɑʒ]（暗中破壞）
		undermine [ˌʌndə`maɪn]（由根基來破壞）
		paralyze [`pærəˌlaɪz]（使整個癱瘓）

Exercise 11

請將畫線部分替換成較精緻的文字。

1. <u>look back at the past</u> → _____

2. <u>completely change</u> → _____

3. <u>strengthen</u> → _____

4. <u>play</u> the scandal <u>down</u> → _____

5. <u>fight against</u> someone → _____

6. <u>fight against</u> the fire → _____

7. <u>blame</u> someone → _____

8. <u>pass</u> someone's <u>performance</u> （超越） → _____

9. <u>turn in</u> the key → _____

10. <u>suppose</u> I am right → _____

參 考 答 案

（以下答案只是參考，讀者可由書本中找出更多的進階用法）

1. recall

2. transform

3. intensify

4. dilute

5. confront

6. withstand

7. condemn

8. overshadow

9. submit

10. presume

換成高手用字 4 —動詞片語：

因為動詞非常重要，所以我們寫作時也常用動詞片語來表達。請讀者比較之後，努力熟記，讓它成為自己的寫作資產。

中文	常使用的英文	這樣較精緻
有明亮的前景	have a bright future	expect broad prospects
提出意見	give opinions	air views
		voice opinions
放寬限制	loosen limits	ease restrictions
提出……問題	ask the question about	raise the issue of
對……有影響力	have influence on	wield influence over
寄望於……	put one's hope on	peg one's hope to
使希望破滅	break the hope	shatter the hope
		dampen the hope
		disillusion
擺脫……	get away from…	dissociate oneself from…
消除歧見	stop different opinions	iron out conflicts

對……施壓	put pressure on…	exert pressure on
到最高點	go to the top	reach the zenith
獲利	make money	reap profit
儲存能量	save power	gather momentum
守信用	keep a promise	honor a pledge
有權去……	have rights to…	be entitled to
發起抗爭	start a fight with	lodge a protest against
不顧……的面子	don't care about the face of…	disregard 某人的 sensibilities

換成高手用字 5—名詞

中文	常使用	這樣較精緻
在……方面	side	respect
		aspect
		dimension
光輝	light	radiance
		brilliance
		glow
幻想、幻覺	imagination	illusion [ɪˋljuʒən]
		fantasy
		reverie [ˋrɛvərɪ]
		mirage [məˋrɑʒ]
工具、手段	tool	means（方法）
		instrument（工具、方法）
		implement [ˋɪmpləmənt]（手段、方法）
煩惱	worry	apprehension
		misgiving(s)（可數名詞）

故事	story	plot（強調故事內容） **例**：This movie has a sad plot. anecdote（軼事） legend（傳說）
甜言蜜語	sweet talk	blandishments [`blændɪʃmənts]
細節	details	particulars elaborations
重點	point(s)	essential(s) gist(s) [dʒɪst] focal point(s)
動力	power	impetus [`ɪmpətəs] momentum [mo`mɛntəm]
關聯	relationship	context [`kantɛkst] connection
視野	view	vista [`vɪstə] vision
活力	energy	vitality [vaɪ`tælətɪ] dynamics [daɪ`næmɪks]

會議	meeting	symposium [sɪmˋpozɪəm]（大會）
		forum（論壇）
		seminar（座談會）
		conference（大會）
		assembly（大會）
		conclave [ˋkɑnklev]（秘密會議，尤其教宗選舉）
地位	position	status（身分、地位）
喊人	call	beckon（用手勢喊人）
		summon（傳喚）
情形	situation	scenario [sɪˋnɛrɪ͜o]
玩笑	joke	prank（也可指「惡作劇」）
		zest
談話	talk	dialogue
層面	level	dimension
		facet [ˋfæsɪt]
標準	standard	criterion [kraɪˋtɪrɪən]（複數形是criteria）

變化	change	transformation（徹底的改變）
		cataclysm [ˋkætəͺklɪzəm]（劇變）
		reform（改革）
旁觀者	watcher	onlooker
對未來的展望	future	outlook
方法	way method	means（方法）
		strategy（策略）
		maneuver [məˋnuvɚ]（策略）
		implement（手段）
		scheme（計謀）
		mechanism [ˋmɛkəͺnɪzəm]（機制）
請求	ask	request
		plea

Exercise 12

請將下列文字替換成較精緻的文字。

動詞片語

1. give opinions → _____

2. ask the question about → _____

3. get away from （擺脫） → _____

4. go to the top → _____

5. keep a promise → _____

名詞

6. sweet talk → _____

7. worry → _____

8. energy → _____

9. level → _____

10. big change → _____

參 考 答 案

1. air views

2. raise the issue of

3. dissociate oneself from

4. reach the zenith

5. honor a pledge

6. blandishments

7. apprehension

8. vitality

9. dimension

10. transformation

換成高手用字 6 —副詞

　　副詞的力量很大，只要用得靈巧，往往一個字就代替了一整句話，所以讀者如果要寫進階英文，就須流利地使用副詞。我替各位準備了以下這些副詞，它們對高級英文寫作大有助益。

好像是	seemingly 例 That girl seems frustrated, and she doesn't talk. 　　↓ 改為 That **seemingly** frustrated girl remains quiet.
靠一己之力	single-handedly 例 He caught the thief all by himself. 　　↓ 改為 He **single-handedly** caught the thief.
明確地	specifically 例 He made it very clear that he would like to order that dish. 　　↓ 改為 He **specifically** ordered that dish. 　　　　　　　　　　　　　　　　那道菜
斷然地	categorically [ˌkætə`gɔrɪklɪ]; flatly; sternly 例 She refused his proposal without hesitation. 　　↓ 改為 She **flatly** refused his proposal. 　　　　　　　　　　　　　　　　求婚

名義上來說	nominally [`nɑmənlɪ] 例 You can say that he is the master of dancing. ↓ 改為 He is **nominally** the dancing master. 他是名符其實的舞蹈大師。
令人懷舊地	nostalgically [nɑ`stældʒɪkəlɪ] 例 When I saw this town, I couldn't help but think of the old days, which made me cry. ↓ 改為 This town **nostalgically** brought me to tears.
相反地	contrarily [`kɑntrərɪlɪ] 例 I thought he loved her; on the contrary, he hated her. ↓ 改為 Instead of loving her, he **contrarily** hated her.
在意料之中地	unsurprisingly 例 As we all expected, he married her. ↓ 改為 **Unsurprisingly**, he married her.
在物質上來說	materialistically 例 Even though he is rich, he is not happy. ↓ 改為 He is **materialistically** rich, yet spiritually poor.

不甘願地	reluctantly 例 Even though he didn't want to go, he still went. ↓ 改為 He **reluctantly** went.
再三地	repeatedly 例 I've told them over and over again not to touch that. ↓ 改為 I've **repeatedly** warned them to stay away from it.
本質上來說	essentially 例 The English language itself is quite interesting. ↓ 改為 English is **essentially** interesting.
令人注目地	conspicuously 例 That neon sign is so bright that draws everyone's attention. ↓ 改為 That neon is **conspicuously** bright.
不需爭辯的事實	indisputably 例 He is so generous that no one would argue it. ↓ 改為 He is **indisputably** generous.

量很可觀地	substantially 例 I've cut down the money I spend. ↓ 改為 I've **substantially** reduced my expenses.
明確地說	explicitly 例 He explained very clearly the reasons why we must work hard. ↓ 改為 He **explicitly** indicated the reasons we must work hard.
暗示性地說	implicitly 例 He tried to ask her out, but he didn't say it clearly. ↓ 改為 He **implicitly** asked her out.
比較起來	comparatively 例 Among all the girls, she is especially tall. ↓ 改為 She is **comparatively** tall among all the girls.
依數據上來看	statistically 例 According to statistics, global warming is becoming worse. ↓ 改為 **Statistically**, global warming is worsening.

依事實上來看	realistically 例 It is true that many people aren't happy. ↓ 改為 **Realistically**, many people aren't happy.
令人鼓舞的是	encouragingly 例 He finally succeeded, which encouraged many people. ↓ 改為 **Encouragingly**, he finally succeeded.
令人灰心的是	discouragingly 例 They didn't show up, which discouraged many people. ↓ 改為 **Discouragingly**, they didn't show up.
難以避免地	inevitably; unavoidably 例 Living in this dirty city, he finally got sick. ↓ 改為 He **inevitably** got sick living in this polluted city.
以藝術的角度來看	artistically 例 Even though it is second-hand, it looks beautiful from the point of view of art. ↓ 改為 It is second-hand yet **artistically** beautiful.

以科學的角度來看	scientifically 例 It has been proven by science. ↓ 改為 It has been **scientifically** proven.
理論上來說	theoretically 例 The theory may be right. ↓ 改為 It's **theoretically** correct.
假設說	hypothetically 例 Your suggestion may be helpful, but it's only a hypothesis. ↓ 改為 Your suggestion is **hypothetically** helpful.
從觀念上來看	conceptionally 例 Many Chinese people think that Confucianism is very important. ↓ 改為 **Conceptionally**, many Chinese people esteem Confucianism.

從宗教的觀點來看	religiously 例 According to Christianity, people should love their enemies. 　　　↓ 改為 **Religiously** speaking, Christians should love their enemies.
在傳統上	traditionally 例 It's a Chinese tradition to be nice to parents. 　　　↓ 改為 **Traditionally**, Chinese esteem filial piety. 　　　　　　　　　　　　　　　　孝道
由歷史的角度上來看	historically 例 China has gone through many wars. 　　　↓ 改為 **Historically**, China has been war-ridden.
如夢似幻地	dreamily 例 She danced with him, which was like a dream to her. 　　　↓ 改為 **Dreamily**, she danced with him.

難以下決定地	hesitantly
	例 He couldn't make up his mind if he ought to tell him the bad news or not, but he finally hold him.
	↓ 改為
	Hesitantly, he informed him of the bad news.
基本上	fundamentally
	例 Love and trust are the most basic and important elements of marriage.
	↓ 改為
	Love and trust are **fundamentally** important to marriage.
只是臆測地、推理地	speculatively
	例 Experts are guessing that the economy will recover in Q3.
	↓ 改為
	Speculatively, experts indicate that the economic recovery may arrive in Q3.
	（※ Q3 = the third quarter 第三季）

Exercise 13

請運用副詞重新撰寫句子。

1. That girl looks happy, and she loves dancing.

答案：＿＿＿＿＿＿＿＿＿＿＿＿＿＿＿＿＿＿＿＿

2. They didn't tell anyone but her the good news.

答案：＿＿＿＿＿＿＿＿＿＿＿＿＿＿＿＿＿＿＿＿

3. People call him an expert, but he's just an amateur.

答案：＿＿＿＿＿＿＿＿＿＿＿＿＿＿＿＿＿＿＿＿

4. Even though he is not interested in washing dishes, he still washed them.

答案：＿＿＿＿＿＿＿＿＿＿＿＿＿＿＿＿＿＿＿＿

5. She is very tall, which often draws people's attention.

答案：＿＿＿＿＿＿＿＿＿＿＿＿＿＿＿＿＿＿＿＿

6. She has tried twice to remind him.

答案：＿＿＿＿＿＿＿＿＿＿＿＿＿＿＿＿＿＿＿＿

7. In the real life, most married couples aren't happy.

答案 : _____

8. We assume that is correct.

答案 : _____

9. Even though he couldn't make up his mind about whether he should quit his job, he finally quit.

答案 : _____

10. He wasn't sure if he was correct, but he still made a conclusion with what he knew.

答案 : _____

（以下答案只是參考，讀者可由書本中找出更多的進階用法）

1. That seemingly happy girl loves dancing.

2. They specifically informed her of the good news.

3. He's nominally an expert but actually an amateur.

4. Reluctantly, he washed the dishes.

5. She is conspicuously tall.

6. She has implicitly reminded him twice.

7. Realistically, successful marriages are rare.

8. That is hypothetically correct.

9. He hesitantly resigned.

10. Speculatively, he drew a conclusion.

Exercise 14

一. 試著將紅字部分換成另外的字吧!

1. 她說話清楚。

She speaks clearly.

↓改成

_____

2. 他看起來心情很好。

He looks very happy.

↓改成

_____

3. 我需要一個詳細的報告。

I need a detailed report.

↓改成

_____

4. 我是個過時的老太太。

I'm an old-fashioned older woman.

↓改成

_____

5. 我們的想像力被教育制度限制了。

Our imaginations have been limited by the educational system.

↓改成

_____

6. 他的幽默感是天生的。

He was born with a sense of humor.

↓改成

_____

7. 這是基本的要求。

This is the basic requirement.

↓改成

_____

8. 中國飽受戰爭之苦。

China has suffered from wars.

↓改成

_____

9. 她以家庭為主。

She puts her family first.

↓改成

_____

10. 我們必須加強他的注意力。

We must improve his concentration.

↓改成

_____

二. 改寫句子

1. 我們中國人習慣在過年的時候放鞭炮。

We Chinese are accustomed to setting off firecrackers to celebrate Chinese New Year.

↓

答案：_____

2. 他一直避免談論這個話題。

He tries not to talk about this topic.

↓

答案：_____

3. 第八屆選美比賽將在一個非常美麗的國家公園舉行。

The 8th-annual beauty contest will take place in a very beautiful national park.

↓

答案：_____

4. 你好沒禮貌，真讓我丟臉。

You are so rude that you've made me lose face.

↓

答案：＿＿＿＿＿＿＿＿＿＿＿＿＿＿＿＿＿＿＿＿＿＿

5. 他雖然在國家位居要職，卻失職了。

Even though he has an extremely important position in the country, he didn't do a good job.

↓

答案：＿＿＿＿＿＿＿＿＿＿＿＿＿＿＿＿＿＿＿＿＿＿

6. 我們城市的人口很少，所以人力短缺。

The population is very small in our city; therefore, we are short of labor.

↓

答案：＿＿＿＿＿＿＿＿＿＿＿＿＿＿＿＿＿＿＿＿＿＿

7. 她天生就是音樂家。

She was born to be a musician.

↓

答案：＿＿＿＿＿＿＿＿＿＿＿＿＿＿＿＿＿＿＿＿＿＿

8. 這是一個紀錄片，內容是舉例說明世界暖化的危機。

This documentary demonstrates the crisis of global warming with examples.

↓

答案：_____

9. 在這最重要的時刻，她失蹤了！

She disappeared at the most important time!

↓

答案：_____

10. 他毫無保留地展現對她的愛，使她流下淚來。

He fully displayed his love for her, making her cry.

↓

答案：_____

1. explicitly

2. elated

3. elaborated

4. obsolete

5. confined

6. He has a natural sense of humor.

7. fundamental

8. war-ridden

9. She is family-oriented.

10. intensity

1. Traditionally, Chinese set off firecrackers during the Lunar New Year.

2. He is shunning this issue.

3. The 8th-annual beauty contest will be staged in a picturesque national park.

4. Your rudeness has disgraced me.

5. He betrayed his indispensible position in the country.

6. Our sparsely-populated city is short of manpower.

7. She is a natural musician.

8. This exemplary documentary alerts us about global warming.

9. She disappeared at a crucial moment.

10. His undisguised love for her brought her to tears.

Unit 10

引用睿智之語
是明智之舉

寫英文作文時，若適時地引用智慧之語，絕對是明智之舉，它對作者的貢獻是：

1. 我們雖然可能平凡，但是引用智慧人的看法，我們的文章也具有智慧。

2. 我們雖然可能平凡，但是各位看看！連如此智慧之人也贊同我的看法，可見我也不算太差！

但是，不用永遠停留在 "A friend in need is a friend indeed." 或 "Make hay while the sun shines." 的階段。我強烈期盼讀者多背一些詞藻優美、令人眼目一新西方常用的睿智話語，為英文作文增值增色。

為了協助讀者學習，我將可能**有助於英文寫作的智慧之語**做以下的記憶設計：

Part 1

---

1. 十年樹木，百年樹人。

It _花費_ three _代_ to make a _紳士_ .
   takes   generations   gentleman

---

2. 事實勝於雄辯。

_行動_s speak _比較大聲_ than _字_s .
Actions   **louder**   **words**

（※ 英文須活用，"Actions speak louder than words." 亦可用於「身教重於言教」。）

---

3. 木已成舟，為時已晚。

The <u>骰子</u> is <u>被擲出去了</u> .
　　　die　　　　**cast**

（※ cast 的動詞三態同型）

---

4. 言多必失。

The <u>舌頭</u> talks at the <u>腦袋的</u>　<u>成本</u> .
　　　tongue　　　　　　**head's**　**cost**

---

5. 盡人事，聽天命。

<u>男人</u>　<u>謀劃</u> ,　<u>神</u>　<u>處理</u> .
Man proposes god disposes

---

6. 魚與熊掌難以兼得。

<u>留住</u> one's <u>蛋糕</u> and <u>吃掉它</u> , too.
Have　　　　**cake**　　　**eat it**

（蛋糕吃了就留不住了；若要留下蛋糕，則又不能吃。）

---

7. 自己闖天下。

<u>燒</u> a <u>路徑</u> for oneself.
Blaze　**trail**

---

8. 多此一舉。

　帶著　　煤炭　to Newcastle.

Carry　coals

（※ Newcastle 是英國的產煤區）

---

9. 三個和尚沒水喝。

Two is ___作伴___ , three is ___一群人___ .

　　　company　　　　　**a crowd**

（兩個還能作伴，如果人多了，就不那麼親了）

---

10. 殺雞取卵。

Kill the ___鵝___ that _____下金蛋s_____.

　　　　goose　　**lays the golden eggs**

請完成以下常用的智慧語：

1. 盡人事，聽天命。

Man _____, god _____.

2. 十年樹木，百年樹人。

It takes _____ _____ to make a _____.

3. 三個和尚沒水喝。

Two is _____, three is _____ _____.

4. 言多必失。

The _____ talks at the _____ _____.

5. 自己闖天下。

_____ a _____ for _____.

1. proposes / disposes

2. three / generations / gentleman

3. company / a / crowd

4. tongue / head's / cost

5. Blaze / trail / oneself

Part 2

1. 持續到最後的，才是贏家！

He who 笑到最後 , 笑得最久 .

laughs last   laughs longest

2. 人各有所好。

One man's 肉 may be another man's 毒藥 .

meat   **poison**

3. 江山易改，本性難移。

You can't 教 an 老狗 new 把戲 .

teach   old dog   tricks

（※ 亦可說 "A leopard can't change his spots." 花豹改不了斑點。）

4. A和B格格不入。

A and B are like a 方木釘 in a 圓洞 .

square peg   round hole

（※ 亦可說 A & B are like a 圓木釘 in a 方洞。）

5. 聊勝於無。

半條吐司麵包 is better than 啥都沒 .

Half a loaf   **none**

（※ a loaf 是一條吐司麵包；bread 是麵包包括吐司麵包；toast 則是烤過的吐司麵包）

6. 一樣米養百樣人。（這世界無奇不有。）

It takes <u>所有的</u> <u>種類</u> to make a world.
　　　　　all　　sorts

---

7. 好酒沉甕底。

The best <u>魚</u> swim near the <u>底部</u>.
　　　　　fish　　　　　　　bottom

（※ fish 是集合名詞，不加 s，動詞仍使用多數）

---

8. 如人飲水，冷暖自知。

<u>沒人</u> knows where the <u>鞋</u> <u>打腳</u> like the <u>穿的人</u>.
No one　　　　　　　shoe pinches　　　　wearer

---

9. 我內心百感交集。

I'm <u>被纏繞著</u> with <u>一大堆</u> feelings.
　　 tangled　　　　 a multitude of

---

10. 平時不做虧心事，半夜敲門心不驚。

A good <u>良心</u> is a soft <u>枕頭</u>.
　　 conscience　　　　 pillow

請完成以下常用的智慧語：

1. 人各有所好。

One man's _____ may be another man's _____.

2. 平時不做虧心事，半夜敲門心不驚。

A good _____ is a _____ _____.

3. 一樣米養百樣人。

It _____ all _____ to make a _____.

4. 如人飲水，冷暖自知。

_____ knows where the _____ _____ like the _____.

5. 我內心百感交集。

I'm _____ with a _____ of _____.

1. meat / poison

2. conscience / soft / pillow

3. takes / sorts / world

4. No one / shoe / pinches / wearer

5. tangled / multitude / feelings

Part 3

1. 集思廣益。

Two <u>腦袋</u>s are better than one.
    heads

---

2. 深藏不露。（※ 或大智若愚）

<u>靜止的</u> waters run <u>深</u> .
Still   **deep**

（※ waters 表示河水、湖水、海水）

---

3. 名師出高徒。

Like <u>老師</u> , like <u>學生</u> .
  teacher   **pupil**

（※ 或是「笨老師教出笨學生。」）

---

4. 捨近求遠。

<u>追尋</u> far and wide for what <u>躺在手邊</u> .
Seek   **lies close at hand**

---

5. 知足常樂。

<u>滿足</u> is better than <u>財富</u> .
Content   **riches**

6. 酒後易失言。

There's many a 溜掉 between the 嘴巴 and the 杯子 .
                  slip   **mouth**   **cup**

---

7. 醉翁之意不在酒。

Many kiss the 孩子 for the 護士的   緣故 .
                child   **nurse's** **sake**

（※ 藉著探望孩子之便而接近護士。）

---

8. 天下沒有不散的筵席。

Even the 最長的 day must have an 結束 .
           longest   **end**

---

9. 以柔克剛。

A 柔軟的 and 微妙的 approach can 卸除武裝 a man of his 壞脾氣 .
  soft   **subtle**   **disarm**   **hot temper**

---

10. 最危險之處也就是最安全之處。

The 最暗的 place is under the 蠟燭台 .
  darkest   **candlestick**

（※ 蠟燭台上有火光，所以非常明亮，下面卻被燭台擋住了，十分陰暗。）

Exercise 17

請完成以下常用的智慧語：

1. 天下沒有不散的筵席。

Even the longest _____ must have an _____.

2. 以柔克剛。

A soft and _____ _____ can disarm a _____ of his

_____ _____.

3. 最危險之處也就是最安全之處。

The darkest _____ is under the _____.

4. 深藏不露。

Still _____ run _____.

5. 知足常樂。

_____ is better than _____.

1. day / end

2. subtle / approach / man / hot / temper

3. place / candlestick

4. waters / deep

5. Content / riches

Part 4

1. 肚大能容。

The 樹枝s that 生得最多 hang 最低 .
boughs　　　**bear most**　　**lowest**

---

2. 君子之交淡如水，水長流。

A 樹籬 between keeps friendship 青綠 .
hedge　　　　　　　　　　　　**green**

---

3. 吃得苦中苦，方為人上人。

逆境 leads to 繁華 .
Adversity　**prosperity**

---

4. 萬事起頭難。

All things are 難 before they are 容易 .
　　　　　　difficult　　　　　　**easy**

---

5. 不經一事，不長一智。

A 摔跤 into a 坑 , a 收穫 in your 智力 .
　fall　　　**pit**　**gain**　　　　**wit**

---

6. 半瓶水響叮噹。

Empty 容器s make the most 聲音 .
　　　　vessels　　　　　　　　**sound**

---

7. 無風不起浪。

There is no 煙 without 火 . / Where there's 煙 , there's 火 .
　　　　　　smoke　　**fire**　　　　　　　　**smoke**　　　**fire**

---

8. 賠了夫人又折兵。

Went for the 羊毛 , but got 剃毛 .
　　　　　　　wool　　　　　**shorn** (shear-shore-shorn)

（※ 原本去偷羊毛，結果自己被剃毛了！）

---

9. 一失足成千古恨。

One wrong 步 may bring a great 摔跤 .
　　　　　　step　　　　　　　　　**fall**

---

10. 玉不琢，不成器。

The finest 鑽石 must be 切割 .
　　　　　diamond　　　　**cut**

Exercise 18

請完成以下常用的智慧語：

1. 吃得苦中苦，方為人上人。

_____ leads to _____.

2. 萬事起頭難。

All things are _____ before they are _____.

3. 半瓶水響叮噹。

Empty _____ make the most _____.

4. 賠了夫人又折兵。

Went for the _____, but got _____.

5. 玉不琢，不成器。

The _____ diamond must be _____.

1. Adversity / prosperity

2. difficult / easy

3. vessels / sound

4. woul / shorn

5. finest / cut

Part 5

1. 五十步笑百步。

The <u>平底鍋</u> calls the <u>茶壺</u> <u>黑</u>.
     pot   **kettle black**

2. 開卷有益。

Reading is always <u>有助益的</u>.
            beneficial

3. 樂極生悲。

<u>歡樂</u> has a <u>刺</u> in his <u>尾巴</u>.
Pleasure   **sting**   **tail**

4. 水能載舟，亦能覆舟。

The wind that <u>吹熄</u>s the <u>蠟燭</u> also <u>燃起</u>s the <u>火焰</u>.
     blows out   **candle**   **kindles**   **flare**

5. 法網恢恢，疏而不漏。

<u>正義</u> has a long <u>手臂</u>.
Justice   **arm**

6. 近朱者赤，近墨者黑。

Keep good men __同伴__ and you shall be the __數目__ .
　　　　　　　　company　　　　　　　　　　number

（※ 與好人作伴，你就會成為眾數之一份子）

---

7. 羨慕無助於事（羨慕令人心中難受不已）。

__羨慕__ has no __假日__ .
Envy　　　　holidays

---

8. 長江後浪推前浪。

The new __世代__s are __勝過__ the old ones.
　　　　generations　excelling

---

9. 樹大招風。

A tall tree __抓住__es much wind.
　　　　　　catches

---

10. 凡事都是別人錯，自己從不錯。

A bad __工匠__ always __責怪__s his __工具__s .
　　　craftsman　　　blames　　　tools

Exercise 19

請完成以下常用的智慧語：

1. 五十步笑百步。

The _____ calls the _____ black.

2. 羨慕無助於事。

_____ has no _____.

3. 樹大招風。

A _____ _____ catches _____ _____.

4. 水能載舟，亦能覆舟。

The wind that _____ _____ the _____ also _____ the _____.

5. 法網恢恢，疏而不漏。

_____ has a _____ _____.

1. pot / kettle

2. Envy / holidays

3. tall / tree / much / wind

4. blows / out / candle / kindles / flare

5. Justice / long / arm

Part 6

1. 引狼入室。

_安排_ the _狐狸_ to keep the _鵝_ .
Set　　　　**fox**　　　　　　　**geese**

（鵝的單數是 goose ；變化同「牙齒」：tooth → teeth）

2. 不入虎穴，焉得虎子？

Nothing _被冒險_ , nothing _被收穫_ .
　　　　ventured　　　　　　**gained**

3. 小心駛得萬年船。

_小心_ is the _父或母_ of _安全_ .
Caution　　**parent**　　**safety**

4. 一言九鼎。

Promise is _欠債_ .
　　　　　　debt

5. 人人平等，不要歧視人。

A _貓_ may look at the _國王_ .
　cat　　　　　　　　**king**

6. 會欺負人的絕非大丈夫。

A ___惡霸___ is always a ___懦夫___ .
    bully   **coward**

---

7. 本末倒置。

Put the ___馬車___ before the ___馬匹___ .
      cart   **horse**

---

8. 天有不測風雲。

It's the ___無法預知的___ that always happens.
      unforeseen

（※ the＋形容詞＝集合名詞，表示全部。例：the elderly 老人；the weak 衰弱之人；the poor 窮人）

---

9. 事後諸葛。

It's easier to be ___睿智的___ after the ___事件___ .
        wise   **event**

---

10. 冰凍三尺，非一日之寒。

___羅馬___ was not built in a day.
Rome

---

11. 第一印象最重要。

First impressions are ___一半___ the ___作戰___ .
　　　　　　　　　　　　 half　　 **battle**

---

12. 親兄弟，明算帳。

Short ___帳___ make long ___朋友___ .
　　　 accounts　　　　 **friends**

（帳算得勤快，反而有助於友誼）

---

13. 愈得不到的東西愈珍貴。

___被禁止的___ fruit is sweet.
Forbidden

---

14. 巧婦難為無米之炊。

You cannot make ___磚頭s___ without ___稻草___ .
　　　　　　　　 bricks　　　　 **straw**

（※ 古時的磚頭是稻草做成的）

請填寫以下常用的智慧語：

1. 第一印象最重要。

First _____ are _____ the _____.

2. 愈得不到的愈珍貴。

_____ _____ is sweet.

3. 一言九鼎。

_____ is _____.

4. 天有不測風雲。

It's the _____ that _____ _____.

5. 不入虎穴，焉得虎子？

Nothing _____, nothing _____.

6. 人人平等，不要歧視人。

A _____ may look at the _____.

7. 親兄弟，明算帳。

_____ _____ make _____ _____.

8. 引狼入室。

Set the _____ to keep the _____.

9. 本末倒置。

Put the _____ before the _____.

10. 小心駛得萬年船。

_____ is the _____ of _____.

1. impressions / half / battle

2. Forbidden / fruit

3. Promise / debt

4. unforeseen / always / happens

5. ventured / gained

6. cat / king

7. Short / accounts / long / friends

8. fox / geese

9. cart / horse

10. Caution / parent / safety

結 論

　　至此，讀者對於何謂高級英文作文，以及如何寫出高級英文作文，應該已有相當的掌握。學習首重方法，方法不對的話，努力一生皆枉然。在本書結尾之時，我再次強調高級英文作文的特色：

1. 字彙是成熟的。
2. 句子是精湛而且有力的。
3. 邏輯是縝密而且完整的。
4. 架構維持起、承、轉、合的邏輯，而且更靈活。
5. 內涵有深度、有廣度，而且任何的資訊或觀點都具可信度。
6. 文筆是細膩的。
7. 氣勢是磅礴的。
8. 讀後是令人內心迴盪的。

　　不過，「師父領進門，修行在個人。」我期盼讀者細心地研讀，大膽地創作。只要有毅力、有理性、有感情、有邏輯，每一位讀者都可以寫出高級英文作文！

大・師・獨・門
英語學習秘技

無私公開

翻譯大師 教你練口說

翻譯大師 教你記單字 基礎篇

翻譯大師 教你學發音

翻譯大師 教你練聽力

翻譯大師 教你記單字 進階篇

翻譯大師 教你寫出好句子

口筆譯教學與實務第一人郭岱宗教授如是說：
「方法對了，英文自然向上提升」

顛覆不景氣，
贏向新多益！
搭配學習法助你大勝利！

越是不景氣，越是要懂得如何花對錢栽培自己！
買一堆不對的書又看不完，既不環保且沒效率！
新多益900↑分者，教你如何精瘦預算一次就用對高分良冊！

堅定基礎
新多益關鍵字彙本領書／定價380
新多益文法本領書／定價299

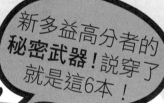

新多益高分者的
秘密武器！說穿了
就是這6本！

800

900

700

提昇實力
新多益閱讀本領書／定價299
新多益聽力本領書／定價299

突破解題
新多益題型透析本領書／定價429
新多益模擬測驗本領書／定價560

國家圖書館出版品預行編目資料

翻譯大師教你學寫作. 高分修辭篇 / 郭岱宗 作.
--初版. -- 台北市：貝塔出版：智勝文化發行, 2010.08
　　面；公分
ISBN 978-957-729-792-1（平裝）
1.英語　2.作文　3.寫作法
805.17　　　　　　　　　　　　　　　　99009066

翻譯大師教你學寫作-高分修辭篇

作　　者 / 郭岱宗
插 畫 者 / 水腦
執行編輯 / 朱慧瑛

出　　版 / 貝塔出版有限公司
地　　址 / 100 台北市館前路 12 號 11 樓
電　　話 / (02) 2314-2525
傳　　真 / (02) 2312-3535
郵　　撥 / 19493777 貝塔出版有限公司
客服信箱 / btservice@betamedia.com.tw

總 經 銷 / 時報文化出版企業股份有限公司
地　　址 / 桃園市龜山區萬壽路二段 351 號
電　　話 / (02) 2306-6842

出版日期 / 2018 年 4 月初版六刷
定　　價 / 260 元
ISBN: 978-957-729-792-1

翻譯大師教你學寫作─高分修辭篇
Copyright 2010 by 郭岱宗
Published by Beta Multimedia Publishing

喚醒你的英文語感！

請對折後釘好，直接寄回即可！

100 台北市中正區館前路12號11樓

 貝塔語言出版 收
Beta Multimedia Publishing

寄件者住址 □□□

貝塔語言出版
Beta Multimedia Publishing

讀者服務專線 (02) 2314-3535 讀者服務傳真 (02) 2312-3535
客戶服務信箱 btservice@betamedia.com.tw
www.betamedia.com.tw

謝謝您購買本書！！
貝塔語言擁有最優良之英文學習書籍，為提供您最佳的英語學習資訊，您填妥此表
後寄回（免貼郵票），將可不定期免費收到本公司最新發行之書訊及活動訊息！

姓名：_____   性別：□男 □女   生日：_____年_____月_____日

電話：（公）_____（宅）_____（手機）_____

電子信箱：_____

學歷：□高中職含以下   □專科 □大學   □研究所含以上
職業：□金融 □服務 □傳播 □製造 □資訊 □軍公教 □出版
　　　□自由 □教育 □學生 □其他
職級：□企業負責人 □高階主管 □中階主管 □職員 □專業人士

1. 您購買的書籍是？_____

2. 您從何處得知本產品？（可複選）
　　□書店 □網路 □書展 □校園活動 □廣告信函 □他人推薦 □新聞報導 □其他_____

3. 您覺得本產品價格：
　　□偏高 □合理 □偏低

4. 請問目前您每週花了多少時間學英語？
　　□不到十分鐘 □十分鐘以上，但不到半小時 □半小時以上，但不到一小時
　　□一小時以上，但不到兩小時 □兩個小時以上 □不一定

5. 通常在選擇語言學習書時，哪些因素是您會考慮的？
　　□封面 □內容、實用性 □品牌 □媒體、朋友推薦 □價格 □其他_____

6. 市面上您最需要的語言書種類為？
　　□聽力 □閱讀 □文法 □口說 □寫作 □其他_____

7. 通常您會透過何種方式選購語言學習書籍？
　　□書店門市 □網路書店 □郵購 □直接找出版社 □學校或公司團購 □其他_____

8. 給我們的建議：_____

_____

_____

喚醒你的英文語感！

Get a Feel for English !